D0507667

Country Life

Country Life

CHARLOTTE
BINGHAM

Michael Joseph
London

First published in Great Britain by Michael Joseph Ltd
44 Bedford Square, London WC1
1985

British Library Cataloguing in Publication Data

Bingham, Charlotte
   Country life.
   I. Title
   823'.914[F]   PR6052.1774

ISBN 0 7181 2531 2

Typeset by Sunrise Setting, Torquay
Printed and bound in Great Britain by
Billing & Sons Ltd, London and Worcester

Time – The Past Imperfect

Chapter One

The Seventh Marchioness of Pemberton looked round her husband's ancestral hall with some satisfaction. It was so much more authentic now that she had added the two reproduction suits of mediaeval armour, and the bronze African shield upon which she hoped Bloss could be persuaded to put the post. Before, well, before you could not have said that this was the hall of a Marquis, but now it had just the right hint of antiquity, for Jennifer had not been a Marchioness long enough not to still take great enjoyment in the fact that her husband's ancestry was impeccable; so old, and so distinguished in fact, that she had now come to regard even the Norman Conquest as almost recent enough for her to have learnt of it on the BBC News.

Perhaps it was because the second anniversary of her wedding was so imminent that she had decided to make the changes in the hall, or perhaps it was because the incessant rain of the past week had confined her to barracks, but whatever the reason there was no doubt that Pember could not but be pleased with her. She knew that he spoiled her quite dreadfully, but she also knew that this was perfectly proper, for he was older than her and she had given him an heir, *the* heir, that he had so wanted; in return she had been given five houses, seven cars, fifteen racehorses and a private art collection which could be kindly loaned. She also had a wishing well, which in light of her material possessions might be considered superfluous but which she herself counted as very precious, for if anyone in the house – such as one of the staff – really irritated her, then she was able to go and sit by her well and wish them all sorts of things that they would not wish themselves.

The staff were one of her greatest causes of anxiety, for she had only to sneeze, or to ladder her tights, or to renew the scent in the potpourri, for the rest of the County to hear about it, and that was the most beastly bore, and something to which she often felt she would never get used. Even now she knew Bloss would be scurrying down to the Queens Arms on his horrid little Honda to tell the landlord of the very recent innovations in the hall, and of the very great inconvenience to himself. Bloss did not enjoy having a châtelaine, as well as – Jennifer paused in her thoughts wondering what the opposite to 'châtelaine' was, but having wasted most of her educational days reading *My Friend Flicka* under her desk, she could not supply the answer and was quite relieved to hear the front doorbell ringing.

Mrs Dupont looked a little taken aback at seeing Jennifer at the door, as if she felt it somewhat lese-majesty for Lady Pemberton to be doing anything so menial, or, knowing Mrs Dupont, more than likely she considered herself so important that only a butler in a nylon coat should open to her. Whichever way it was, Jennifer wished most heartily that she had not bothered to answer the front door, for the very last person that she personally wanted to see on this dreary rainy evening, with her silly fat face peering under her silly little fold-away umbrella, was Jane Dupont, but one of the worst aspects of country life was the fact that you could not be rude to anyone. It was such a strain, but nothing like the strain that was being felt by the buttons on Mrs Dupont's green quilted coat, which were barely holding out against the volumes beneath, and threatened any moment to have to give way to a hideous outbreak of acrylic and viscose.

'Contributions needed for the village hall.'

She held out her collecting box, an old marmalade jar covered with a little frilly paper top, which had a slit in it.

Jennifer stared at her.

'Saving the village hall?'

'Yes, yes, of course.'

Jennifer turned to go back into the hall, and was sorry to see Mrs Dupont following her. She stopped.

'But I thought we saved the village hall last year?'

'Yes, we did,' Mrs Dupont agreed, 'but this is for the Portacabins, for the More Mature. Very urgent. The Vicar is desperate – his Art Classes, you know?'

The Vicar got on Jennifer's nerves. He was the sort of chap that made you doubt God's judgement, since He had chosen the Vicar to follow Him. The Vicar had teeth that were retained with difficulty, and a wife that no one would retain, not even for cleaning silver. And as for his Art Classes, if they were not so damaging to the village and unsettling to everyone, they would be laughable.

'But I thought everyone in the village was against Art Classes, ever since the committee vetoed Mavis Bundage posing for the still-life class?'

'Yes, that was most upsetting, but no, these are quite different classes, watercolour, very suitable, gets everyone together talking in the hall. Makes them feel they're a village.'

Since most of the village was employed in one capacity or another to work on their estate, Jennifer could not see the slightest benefit to the village in their getting together in the village hall. Besides, watercolour classes should be held in the open air with camp stools, and plenty of trees for those in need. There should be absolutely no necessity for anything in the way of Portacabins for the more mature. She could not of course say this to Mrs Dupont, for even though Jennifer was the Seventh Marchioness of Pemberton, she had not been married to the Seventh Marquis for very long, and any criticism she might have of the Vicar, Mrs Dupont, Portacabins or watercolour classes would have to be kept to herself, or the dread criticism would be raised that the big house and its land dominated the village, that it was not proper for this to happen in these modern times, and that Pember's family should not hold the tenancies to so many people's cottages. As it was, during the last election she had counted as many as eight Labour posters behind net curtains, while apparently several people were heard quite blatantly talking about things like Further Education in the pub. Such subjects were only suitable for those who had it, and that certainly did not include the regulars at the Queens Arms. Nevertheless it had made Pember uneasy, and although he had not said anything to her, she had observed that he had subsequently bought some property in Australia, perhaps because it too was Further.

'Did you know that there was a new occupant for Flint House?' asked Mrs Dupont, while Jennifer searched for something a little less ostentatious than a ten-pound note to put in the wretched jar.

'I knew that it was sold, of course, but I didn't know to whom it had been sold to – ' said Jennifer, running into a grammatical as well as a monetary cul-de-sac, for she could not find anything less than the ten-pound note to put in the jar, and that would most certainly be taken wrong, so she folded it as small as was possible, with her back turned away from the wretched woman, and then she popped it in the marmalade pot, while carrying on an eye-to-eye conversation to distract her. It was quite exhausting.

'I thought that somebody had said that Flint House was attracting foreign interest? Yes, I'm quite sure they did.'

'No, by no means, it has been bought by a Lady Tisbury,' said Mrs Dupont with satisfaction.

Not for the first time Jennifer deplored this business of English titles enabling everyone from a Baron's wife to a Marchioness to be called by the same appendage. It was all very well people trilling away at you about 'everyone's a Lord except a Duke', but then quite frankly what was it all about? What was the point in being better than someone else, when the better bit only showed on an envelope, or an invitation? Reform of something or another was needed, but she wasn't quite sure what. Anyway, it was temporarily of secondary interest to the fact that a Lady Tisbury had bought Flint House, for Jennifer had been feeling a little lonely since the baby, and although she saw Pember at breakfast, lunch, and of course dinner, it was really a little unvaried, even for her quiet tastes. Yet there was no question of her associating on an intimate level with someone like Mrs Dupont, because the moment you let a woman like that into your private sitting room all life as you like to think of it would be at an end, of that there was no doubt. But, on the other hand, 'Lady Tisbury' sounded a great possibility. Happily Flint House was so far inferior to the Hall that even should she turn out to be a fellow Marchioness or a concealed Countess, it would be of very little import, for Jennifer knew that there would never be any question of the village fête being held in any but her grounds. Of course she couldn't ask Mrs Dupont anything more relevant about Lady Tisbury, it would not be suitable, so she waited until she had closed the door thankfully behind her, and then ran upstairs to look up 'Tisbury' in that well known Bible of country life – *Debrett's Peerage*.

The new young Lady Tisbury, who had replaced the old ageing Lady Tisbury once she had fallen prey to something fatal in the foothills of the Himalayas, was happily unaware of the village's interest in both her and her new house. All Patti knew was that it was the first house that she had ever lived in, and she was quite determined to make it as lovely as possible. In this she was looking forward to being hopelessly indulged by Sir Gerard, just as he hoped to be equally indulged in other ways.

'Baby's pinch!'

Patti pinched him playfully on the other cheek, trying to fix his attention more firmly on the wallpapers.

'Whatever you think, baby darling, whatever you think.'

'But Big G., it's our home,' said Patti reproachfully.

'I'm a bit old-fashioned. You know how it is.'

'I rather thought the gold-embossed, it would go with the zebra-striped couch, and all my mirrors, don't you think?'

Gerard nodded.

'I know the style. Used to be known as "coo-coo".'

'Did it? Really? So it's really and truly period then?' asked Patti.

'Oh yes, it's really and truly period,' said Gerard, placing a hand on her suede-encased bottom. 'In fact I can honestly say there has never been a time in history when that sort of style hasn't been popular.'

'What, never?' asked Patti.

'No never,' said Gerard, 'not since the Roman times.'

'I never realised it was that period,' said Patti wonderingly.

'Oh it's that period all right,' said Gerard, 'and personally speaking I've always felt very at home with it.'

Patti closed the little fan of samples and put it on the mantelpiece, before he had time to turn them over and see the

5

prices. She wanted her first real home to be everything that it should be, but most of all she definitely wanted it to have a 'period' feel, and if it meant paying a little more for the gold-embossed paper to achieve the 'coo-coo' period look, well, then that was just too bad.

'Hallo? Hallo?' cried a voice from the short carriage drive, and the front door was pushed open by Mrs Dupont, who entered the hall and stood tactlessly rattling her collecting jar for attention.

Patti frowned a smallish frown, for already she was at an age when she had become aware that even the lightest expression could mark the face, and make her less desirable in later life.

Gerard turned to leave her. 'My mama used to say, "Don't talk to anyone in the County until you've seen their visiting cards",' he reminded Patti. 'They only ever call for a reason and it's usually money, you'll find.'

He let himself out of the french windows into the garden, as Patti heard Mrs Dupont calling again from the hall.

'Hallo? Hallo?'

Mrs Dupont's rounds on behalf of the village hall had been exhausting, possibly because she was wearing shoes with slightly raised heels which had become spiked with divots of grass, which she was now walking round Patti's sitting room as unrepentant as some Sunday golfer committing a mis-demeanour in another person's club.

'Do let me introduce myself,' said Mrs Dupont. 'I'm Jane Dupont – how do you do?'

'Hello?' said Patti.

She didn't like the way Mrs Dupont's bronze toning Classic Casuals were cut – pleats on a woman of her size were not attractive – and although she was carrying her green quilted coat over her arm, for it had stopped raining, Patti could see it had a sort of mark on the front, and the pocket was torn.

'Isn't moving ghastly?' said Mrs Dupont, putting down her marmalade collecting jar. 'Worse than anything.'

'I find it very exciting,' said Patti.

'The last time we moved I told my husband if he ever wanted to move again it would be without me.'

'I find it very exciting,' said Patti again.

6

'In the old days of course men went off and shot tigers, now whenever they get restless they move you. Boring, very boring. Still, if they can afford the new carpets and curtains, why not?'

She glanced with feigned disinterest at some swatches of materials on the table by the fireplace and then quickly picked them up.

'Very nice. I love Esmé and Glance myself, and oh, and the Michael Krantz Woodwind Collection. Of course. Very popular.'

'We're not having the velveteen finish,' said Patti quickly.

'No?'

'We're having the Gelber dirt resistant beige mottled –'

'Of course, everyone's having that, on the stairs, of course.'

Mrs Dupont smiled, showing small pointed teeth.

Patti said suddenly, 'Do you have a visiting card?'

'Good heavens no,' said Mrs Dupont, startled. 'Why?'

Patti's smile hadn't been so dazzling since she'd won a competition for Greek dancing at her convent.

'I doubt if you'll find anyone in the whole of England who still leaves a calling card, Lady Tisbury, except of course people in Insurance, and my husband's not in anything like that.'

'You must be very proud of him, then? So few people can escape being in anything nowadays, don't you think?'

Patti sighed.

'Is Sir Gerard in something then?' asked the still-startled Mrs Dupont.

'Yes, I'm afraid my Knightey's in investments,' said Patti sadly.

'I expect you're glad to be in the house at last,' said Mrs Dupont.

She glanced towards the garden outside the floor-length window, where a tattered awning flapped desultorily in the spring breeze, and then she went to the window and stared out at the old path beyond the window, which was so smothered in moss that it had acquired its own velveteen finish.

'The garden, alas, cannot be hurried through like the house,' said Mrs Dupont.

'I'm not much of a person for gardens,' said Patti. 'We only had some Easi-Grow plastic tubs at the flat in London.'

'You're not on clay here,' said Mrs Dupont, 'so, as you know, you will be gardening as for Wiltshire.'

Patti did not know, and she knew that Mrs Dupont knew that she did not know, and so she hesitated for a few seconds wondering whether she wasn't after all being just kind and helpful, for if she had wanted to show Patti up she could have done so very easily.

'I must lend you a little book on gardening. I found it indispensable when I moved here.'

'Thank you very much,' said Patti with caution, 'very kind of you.'

'It's only a paperback,' said Mrs Dupont, 'but it has some quite amusing ideas.'

Patti had no idea that gardening could be 'amusing', and for a second she saw herself, book in one hand and trowel in the other, bent over the flower beds, laughing and smiling.

'You must come to dinner with us when you're more settled,' Mrs Dupont added.

Patti wondered why her being more settled was required for going to dinner with Mrs Dupont, if, as she imagined, Mrs Dupont was herself more settled. It was very strange, and though she would obviously be very grateful for Mrs Dupont's book, at the moment she would like her to go. Of course, if her dear Knightey was here he would say 'Goodbye' very loudly and suddenly, which he had a habit of doing, and which normally she did not appreciate as he usually did it to the daily before she'd quite finished doing the floors, for no better reason than he was feeling randy. But dear Knightey was not here, and so it was up to her to get rid of this large woman in her quilted coat.

'Will you excuse me?' she asked Mrs Dupont. 'I must go and –' she searched for an excuse, 'I must go and speak to my Interior Designer. He's organising the festoons for the dining room, and he wants to know my choice.'

Mrs Dupont held out her marmalade jar.

'For the village hall,' she told her.

Patti found her handbag and seeing a ten-pound note in the jar she matched it; then she watched Mrs Dupont walking back across the lawn, this time to the back gate, her heels spiking more divots on to themselves. They were nearly invisible beneath the tufts by the time she reached the old wall, and the gate which led on to the 'B' road, which was frequented only by small boys on bicycles and tractors returning from the fields, but for which Patti was grateful since they made her feel less isolated than she might otherwise have felt, coming from a penthouse overlooking the noisier part of the Upper Richmond Road, and only a short walk from a bus stop that took you to Piccadilly on a number 9.

She picked up the samples of wallpaper from the mantelpiece. She still wanted the green one from the Woodwind Collection, even if Mrs Dupont had said that 'everyone' was having it. If 'everyone' was having it, it probably meant that it was in good taste, surely? Of course, she had lied to get rid of Mrs Dupont. The designer was not ready and waiting for her in the dining room. He was only now driving to the front door in a metallic white-topped convertible Volkswagen with matching gold-spiked wheels, so it was just as well that Mrs Dupont had elected to exit through the back gate. Patti hurriedly hid her wallpaper samples, because just from looking at the confirmed bachelor who, having climbed out of the car, was now straightening the creases from behind the knees of his trousers and carefully smoothing the cuffs of his shirt so that they turned back on his cashmere sweater with an ironed look, just from looking at him, she had an uneasy feeling that he would not approve of the Woodwind Collection. He would find it too feminine, and that being so she would be forced to throw herself entirely upon his personal taste, which was not always advisable, for she had been told by Sir G. that designers liked to offload their slow sellers on innocent people like herself. So she knew that at all costs she must not appear as naive as she undoubtedly was; and yet, having no taste, how would she know what good taste was? She only thanked heaven that being an ex-dancer she was at home with ginger beers, or 'pansies' as Gerard still insisted on calling them.

'I've just been having coffee with Lady Tisbury,' Mrs Dupont lied to her next port of call, Mrs Paine. 'I must say she's most unlikely.'

Since they both played bridge together twice a week she had

no need to elucidate to Margaret Paine what the precise meaning of 'unlikely' was. If Lady Tisbury was 'unlikely' in the view of Jane Dupont, then there was no doubt she would become a fund of, if not a source of, indoor sport for many a future conversation.

'Really?'

Margaret, who had risen to make Jane Dupont a mug of instant supermarket coffee, immediately sat down again, for if Lady Tisbury had already given Jane Dupont a cup of coffee, then there was thankfully no need for her to do the same.

'Tell me.'

'She's nothing you could describe,' said Mrs Dupont, who had no intention of not describing Lady Tisbury in detail, and at great length.

'For a start she wears suede trousers.'

'*Suede*?'

'Totally suede from top to toe. I can't see her going for brisk walks in those, dear, can you?'

'I'll say not,' Margaret agreed, taking out an undersized cigarette, and purposefully forgetting to offer Jane one.

'And she's much younger than him. And I mean *much*.'

'Unsuitably young?' asked Margaret, beginning to cough slightly on her low-tar smoke.

'Totally unsuitably young,' Jane confirmed.

They both looked at each other through Margaret's smoke, each one wondering whom would be the first to go from first gear to top? They both already had a growing picture of 'Lady Tisbury'. A grasping person (anyone younger than her husband by thirty years was automatically grasping), of unsuitable taste, obviously not a country woman, and definitely not someone who would fit in with the rest of the village, if only because she wore suede trousers and put a ten-pound note ostentatiously in the collecting jar.

It had already been very amusing when the farrier had let them know that she was afraid of horses, but now that Mrs Dupont was in command of the fact that she knew nothing about gardening, except that she had once been the proud owner of some Easi-Grow tubs, it was hilarious.

'What's she going to do down here?' asked Margaret, when

they had stopped laughing. 'Of course, she might play bridge?'

'She might,' Jane Dupont said, 'but somehow I doubt it. Looking at her I'd say she was definitely a girl who was proficient at Indoor Sports, but somehow I rather doubt whether they would include bridge.'

'What is she going to do down here, then?'

'We shall see. Ah well, I must be on my way, my dear.'

'Sweet of you to call.'

Mrs Dupont held out her marmalade jar pointedly as she reached Margaret Paine's door. After all, even if she did not want her to offer a coffee, she was not going to let her get away with not putting tenpence in the kitty for the Portacabins.

'Oh dear, no cornices. We'll have to tent it, I'm afraid, Lady Tisbury. It's a must for tenting, I would say.'

'I was wondering about that reproduction plastic moulding – you know?' asked Patti, holding out a much fingered copy of *Interiors*.

Fulton sighed out loud. He had not been looking forward to this visit, so much so that even after he had taken Lady Tisbury's call he had been forced to look her husband up in a reference book, just in case he turned out to be someone a little 'de trop', even for his ever-so recently set up Interior Decoration business. However, to his surprise – and it was surprise – he had found that 'Sir Gerard' was, on paper anyway, perfectly acceptable, and so here he was – le voilà. At least the line-up in the small area in front of the house, that Lady Tisbury rather comically referred to as 'the drive', at least that was most reassuring, consisting as it did of one Porsche, one customised Mini, and one rather-too-new Range Rover.

'I don't think we shall be happy with anything plastic,' said Fulton, pronouncing it 'plarstic'.

'Do you think, though, do you think that Sir Gerard will like eating in a tent?' asked Patti, doubtfully.

'I should say particularly, since he's ex-Army,' said Fulton, who had not done his research for nothing.

He did so hate Victorian villas really, whatever anyone said, but now that he was here, on the other hand, he realised that Flint House would offer a considerable, but agreeable, challenge to him. Not only that, but the knowledge that the Tisburys could afford to be not just pleated, but ruched and draped, knocked through and altogether refurbished, according to his own taste, had given him a tiny little lift. He was so bored with looking for demi-lunes for old ladies; a challenge was just what the boy needed. (Although looking at the Tisburys' furniture he could foresee several obstacles on the horizon.)

'I have a really lovely zebra-striped couch that I bought with Sir Gerard that I want to make part of the sitting room design.'

Fulton's optimism suddenly started to fade.

'I think we might leave the drawing room until another time,' he said hurriedly. 'I could bring you some samples.'

'Sir Gerard favours the coo-coo look. You know?'

'Oh dear, Lady Tisbury, you are funny. Now I must fly. We'll be in touch.'

Fulton hurried to his car. He couldn't wait to get back to Bath and tell Elliott all about Lady Tisbury, and her 'coo-coo' look.

Waiting for Bloss to withdraw after serving dinner was Jennifer's worst moment, particularly if she had something vitally unimportant but fun to tell Pember that Bloss must not hear. She sometimes thought he must have a sort of sixth sense, and took such agonising long minutes to push things through the door on the heated trolleys to the kitchen just to annoy her. Such long minutes that it made the back of her knees ache, the way they used to when she was at school and waiting for the teams to be announced; that's exactly how it was when she wanted to tell Pember something unimportant. Not that Pember would be interested, although she always hoped that he would be, that she would suddenly see the true light of involvement in his eyes instead of just a tolerant 'anything you say dear' kind of look. But there it was, you couldn't be married to someone rich and kind and have them interesting as well.

'Do you know anyone called Tisbury, Pember?'

Pemberton, after three-quarters of a bottle of Château des Gauliers 1947 not only didn't know anyone called 'Tisbury', but he very much cared less. Women had a habit of springing names and places on a chap just when a chap was enjoying himself, and then getting irritated because he couldn't help out.

'Know a station called Tisbury,' he volunteered, and then gazed fondly past the silver peacocks in the middle of the mahogany table to where Jennifer's bosom was supporting his grandmother's garnets and pearls. He liked to reflect, often and contentedly, on the changes he had wrought in his young wife. It was a wonderful thing what a great deal of money could do for a girl's appearance; for his wife when he had met her had resembled nothing more nor less than a knitting pattern, of the kind that would only be picked out by retired nannies, and women who remembered the First World War. Now, although still by no means a beauty, she was a handsome sight, and could most definitely win classes under saddle.

'No Pember sweetie, I'm quite sure they have nothing to do with a station; no, these are people newly arrived in the village – Sir Gerard and Lady Tisbury. They've only just moved into Flint House. Remember? It was on the market? Well, they bought it.'

There was a small silence while Pemberton contemplated this fact, and then realising that something was expected of him he said, 'I see.' He said it twice, because he didn't.

'I thought we ought to ask them up,' Jennifer went on patiently. 'After all, we must be grateful that someone nice has bought it, mustn't we?'

Pemberton couldn't see this at all, all he could see was that Jennifer was hell-bent on socialising, something which was anathemetic to him.

'You're not thinking of giving a party or something?' he asked, suddenly panic-struck.

Jennifer sighed. 'Of course not, Pember sweetie, as if I would, knowing you, and how much you like seeing people, as if I'd give a party.'

'You've re-arranged the hall.'

'Re-arranging the hall is not giving a party, now is it?'

'I don't know, thought you might be suffering a sea-change.'

'We can't always ignore the village you know, much as I know you would like to,' said Jennifer lightly.

'I suppose you're right, you always are,' said Pemberton, 'but I do so like to have you to myself, you know that.'

'You can share me for one little hour with the Tisburys, can't you?'

'All right, but not a minute longer, mind? I don't want them staying to lunch, or any of that kind of thing. I'm sorry, but it can't be helped, and there we are.'

Jennifer rose from the table. She liked to get her own way, so since she just had, she smiled and Pember, who always stayed behind with the port even when they dined alone (probably because they always dined alone), also rose to his feet, but before she could leave the dining room he took her hand and kissed it, deeply, because he was suddenly very grateful, which was what he was meant to be.

On her own in her dear little sitting room, Jennifer dialled Flint House. The ringing tone was as clear as if she was dialling the gate lodge. At length someone answered it; since it was a girl's voice it was obviously not Sir Gerard.

'Lady Tisbury?'

Jennifer had to raise her voice to be heard above the sound of pop playing in the background. At least she thought it must be pop, for it was loud, and Lady Tisbury, if it was she, had also to shout to be heard above it.

'Speaking.'

'Lady Pemberton from the Hall.'

'Hi.'

Jennifer stared at the receiver as if the line had crackled. She had never, in the two years that she had been at the Hall, heard the telephone say 'hi' before. Now what had seemed a perfectly straightforward social manoeuvre was turning into a nightmare.

'I was wondering if you and Sir Gerard would like to come for a drink – on Sunday morning?'

'That sounds great. If you hold on a tick I'll ask Knightey.'

A hand now covered the receiver, a ghastly piece of manners, and then the receiver was again exposed.

'That would be great, thanks a lot.'

Jennifer took a deep breath, such as Betty Parsons had taught her to take in the first stages of childbirth, in other words an intake of air destined to take one's mind off extreme pain.

'We can expect you around noon then?'

'Yes, that would be great. Thanks a lot. Really. Thanks.'

'We shall look forward to it,' said Jennifer.

She replaced the receiver, and then gazed at it in a way that was reminiscent of a hooked trout. No, it really was a nightmare. The only time she took it into her head to ask someone, well not even just a someone, a 'Lady Tisbury', up to the Hall, she turned out to be not at all what Pember – who was anti-social enough, goodness knows – she turned out to be not at all what he would like. And the worst of it all, it being Friday evening and Sunday noon only a day and a half away, it would seem that there was not even enough time to contract a bad case of anything except discourtesy should she telephone to cancel. There was only one real course open to her, and that was to be 'surprised'.

She quickly picked up her needlework, as she could hear Pember's footsteps approaching from the dining room. Yes, that was the only answer. If Pember was horrid or grumbled to her afterwards, she would be incredibly 'surprised'. After all, there was no proof of any kind whatsoever that she had spoken to Lady Tisbury personally, so Pember could not accuse her of a social gaffe in asking her, for she could plead innocence not ignorance; not like that ghastly first dinner party just after she was married when she had told Blos to lay side plates, and Pember had had them publicly removed just as the guests had sat down, and there was no conversation whatsoever to cover his loud 'What the devil are these, Bloss?' No, no, that was not going to happen again, not ever. She plunged her needle into the canvas.

There was no mistaking Lady Tisbury's arrival, for the metal tips of her high-heeled boots rang on the worn flagstones of the hall floor, making a sound reminiscent of forks being dropped. Her shiny belt competed with her lip gloss for attention, which in turn vied with the new gold necklace set with small diamonds which encircled her throat. She had difficulty picking up one of the salted almonds laid out for cocktail snacks, because her wedding ring was sharing its berth with a large solitaire diamond, of the kind that is frequently advertised in the Sunday supplements. Standing beside Sir Gerard in her black leather jodhpurs, into which she had tucked a black silk blouse inset with plunging lace vee, she was a shimmering advertisement for young flesh.

Jennifer, whose face had assumed a permanent flush since Lady Tisbury's entrance, felt so sorry for her that she would have given anything for Patti to go away. Old houses could be dreadfully withering, contemptuous of new fashion, old mores dressed as new mores. Nothing that was not classic could withstand the soft glow that came from the furniture, the paintings, the rugs or the silver, and Jennifer knew this as much as anyone, for at first she herself had lost out hopelessly within the Hall's ancient spotlight.

Sir Gerard, on the other hand, looked as if he might own the place. His face was cragged with the kind of breeding that speaks of hundreds of years of carefully trained dissipation. His chin a little absent, his nose omnipresent, his eyes careless with a look that had seen everything and learnt nothing. He had a natural voice, such as Pember sported, without anything affected in its tones. He mispronounced words with aplomb, and he drank his gin and tonic without ice. In short he was, as Jennifer could see, a gentleman.

'You must be very sad that hunting's nearly over, Sir Gerard,' said Jennifer conversationally.

'I hear you don't,' said Sir Gerard heavily.

'No, I am afraid I am merely someone who hacks,' agreed Jennifer.

'Hacking's sissy. Hacking don't stir the blood.'

Jennifer smoothed her skirt over her knees. Obviously, from just one glance at Lady Tisbury, Sir Gerard was an ardent believer in 'stirring' the blood, something which possibly, again from looking at Lady Tisbury, he would have no trouble whatsoever in doing when her ladyship was around. She was very glad that her Pember was not like that, that he didn't share Sir Gerard's attitude to life, for he was really rather like someone you read about in the Sunday papers. Happily, judging from what she remembered from the reference books, his first wife was dead – and just as well, for if the poor woman had had the bad luck to have lived to see her husband's taste in second wives, no doubt she would have passed away again. What it was that men saw in girls like that she would never

16

know. They smelt of perfume, not scent, and they reeked of lust. And then they so often had a too sudden laugh, or a way of looking at men which hinted at something that would make any decent person such as Pember feel more than a little embarrassed, which was probably why he was now offering to show the wretched girl round the house.

Jennifer smiled vaguely at Sir Gerard, offered him a nut, and then contemplated the difficulty of finding a new subject which was safe, and not about anything which either of them could despise each other for either doing, or not doing, always difficult in the country where even the mention of a play by Bernard Shaw could bring about charges of extreme radicalism.

'I understand you are doing great things at Flint House, Sir Gerard?'

'Yes, builders everywhere,' agreed Gerard, and stared into Jennifer's rounded face so fiercely that for a moment she imagined that he thought she was responsible. 'Women's palaver.'

'But terribly exciting,' said Jennifer.

'Patti's got some frightful pansy tenting everything, it's making me feel like a boy scout.'

'Tenting? But that's all the rage.'

'It's certainly getting me in one,' grumbled Sir Gerard.

'I have to tell you that I wanted to tent our dining room, but my husband forbade it,' said Jennifer.

'Sensible fellow. Trouble is don't make any difference to Patti.'

'What, what don't – doesn't – make any difference to her?'

'What I say, a nod's as good as a wink to a blind pony. Still, so long as she stays in shape, that's all that matters.'

His eyes drifted from Jennifer's cashmere suit with lace collar and pearl necklace to his wife's flashing lips and black vee as she re-entered the drawing room. His expression changed from disinterest to vivid sensuality, and he rose with ill-disguised relief declaring their mutual gratitude for the Pembertons' kind invitation, and their intention of returning the compliment as soon as possible, but to Jennifer's amazement Pember would have none of it. They must stay for another drink, he insisted,

17

and himself poured the drinks. This was unheard of, and Jennifer could only attribute his change of attitude to the fact that he was so terribly kind that he didn't want Sir Gerard to think that they could only take an hour of their company, for in the now nearly two years of their marriage Pember had never once poured a third drink for anyone, or insisted on their staying another minute. He must most definitely be moved by pity and kindness. It was quite touching.

With their eventual departure and the arrival of lunch Jennifer could only feel the most enormous relief, and she went into the dining room still pink-cheeked from her efforts with Sir Gerard, whose conversational expertise could only be compared to a dancing elephant.

Of course once Bloss had finished serving she would apologise to poor Pember about the Tisburys. It was all her silly fault, and she promised herself she would never ever ask anyone to the Hall without previously meeting them. They were, the Tisburys were, perfectly frightful, and there was no getting around that one. He so dissipated, and she so common.

Bloss was still serving the soup when Pemberton looked across at Jennifer, and smiled, and it was not his normal sort of smile, it was the one that he occasionally displayed when they passed one of those shops that sold hideous scanties, and see-through red lace nighties.

'I say – how about that Lady Tisbury? Isn't she a sweetie? Loved her blouse. You must get one like that. What a smasher.'

Happily for Jennifer her Betty Parsons breathing was by now an ingrained habit. She breathed in, deeply. How useful it was for any kind of pain.

Chapter Two

The Countess lay back against her cream lace pillows, and gazed at the still bare trees of the square below. Because it was only early spring she still followed her winter habit of spending a large part of the morning reclining in her bed, and saving on her central heating system. During these mornings, if she was in a realistic mood, she read *The Times* leader, and then having tired of it she would lay her hands on the lace inset of the sheet in front of her and contemplate the ageing process, remembering how in former days when she did the same thing her hands would appear as smooth and as white as the Irish linen upon which her palms rested. And then she would read the second leader, as if by this procedure she would punish herself for growing older.

Today she was not in a realistic mood, and so her hands were inside the sheet, and she had not even opened *The Times* which lay on the Lord Roberts workshop breakfast tray at the bottom of the bed. Instead her eyes turned towards the scene below where London's slow jog towards spring appeared about to result in a few leaves emerging in a seemingly reluctant colour wash of eau de nil. Once she had bored of this backdrop her eyes turned accusingly towards her telephone, white, plastic, and sixtyish, like a lot of her friends, but unlike them unusually silent.

There were two things in her social life that she found insupportable. One was being in demand, and the other was not being in demand. Last week she had been out every night, this week she was in every night. It was thoroughly unsatisfactory. Last week she had instructed the girl (her new concession to moving with the times was to call her 'the girl' rather than 'the maid', which sounded if anything a little American nowadays.) She had instructed 'the girl' to take messages for most of the mornings, because she was so busy; this week the telephone was so silent she felt like ringing up the 'Recipe of the Week' and pretending it was one of her friends. To be in town alone and bored was positively distressing. At her age she had a pressing obligation to enjoy herself, and it was impossible to do that if one was on one's own.

Beautifully timed, the front door bell rang, and she could hear – eventually, for 'the girl' was large, slow, and fat – she could hear her answering it. It couldn't be Harrods, thought the Countess with relief, because they only called on Wednesdays, and it couldn't be a meter man, because they only called when normal people were still asleep, so it had to be someone she knew, and possibly, which would be exciting, someone she had not seen for a long time, or they would have been in touch by telephone. Whoever it was, it was quite clear from the sound of heavy breathing as they climbed the stairs that they were dreadfully out of condition.

Andrew Gillott puffed into the room in answer to her 'Come in'. He smelt revoltingly of cigarettes, and he was looking pudgy-white, even though he had just got back from Africa.

'Andrew,' said the Countess, 'what a surprise.'

And she meant it, because it was.

'Sit down,' she commanded.

Andrew did so, on her small Colefax and Fowler chintz chair. He looked ridiculous because it was only a bedroom chair, and not made to take a silly fat fellow such as he.

'Had to come and see you. Had to,' said Andrew.

'You can't have lost all your dibs again?' asked the Countess, getting straight to what was usually the cause of his troubles.

He shook his head. He wished he had, anything was preferable to his present hell. He lit a cigarette, oblivious to the fact that the Countess immediately picked up a handkerchief and held it to her nose.

'I can't take another day of it.'

'What can't you take another day of?' asked the Countess, vaguely dreading the reply.

'The Mu-Mu Maiden.'

'Clarissa?' asked the Countess, feigning surprise. 'Whatever can you mean? You can only have been married to her for three weeks.'

The Countess got out of bed, and pushed her feet into a pair of slim gold sandals, for lying in bed during this scene gave her the feeling that she was a patient, and Andrew some demented doctor, whereas it was somewhat the other way round.

'Andrew. It's only three weeks since I waved you off to Kenya for your honeymoon, what on earth has been happening? I told you not to go to Kenya for your honeymoon. It's far too far for an old fool like you. It only suits people who like dressing up in safari suits to use their Polaroids. But be that as it may, this is no reason to have hysterics. You've probably just damaged your liver with too much wine, most of our feelings are completely dominated by "la fois", and yours is probably as green as a gooseberry.'

She said all this in answer to her own questions, and making little room for anyone else to reply, even if they should have wanted to, which Andrew quite obviously didn't, for he merely lay back in the little chintz chair and stared in despair at the ceiling which was painted a tasteful peach. His bedroom ceiling, or rather his wife Clarissa's bedroom ceiling, was decorated with large yellow cabbage roses that actually looked like cabbages, and which every time he opened his eyes seemed to smile down at him rank with vulgarity, and no doubt, if he had been able to get close to them, which mercifully he could not, they would smell of Woollies best scent, as she always seemed to, whatever the fragrance she was wearing.

'Have you been to the doctor?' asked the Countess, rather in the manner of matron enquiring whether he was 'regular'.

Andrew put his hand in his pocket to take out another life-saving gasper. He had never felt so in need of nicotine.

'Not another in the bedroom please,' said the Countess crisply. 'This is not the top of a bus. Have you been to the doctor?' she asked again.

'Doctor can't do anything about the Mu-Mu Maiden, except give her a lethal dose, and I don't know that even a private doctor would do that, would he?'

'What about her, what about Mu-Mu mummy, or whatever you call her, have you talked over whatever it is you don't like about her, with her? I mean the one thing Clarissa can do is talk, eternally, and infernally.'

'She's revolting,' groaned Andrew, and started to feel a lump appearing in his throat at the very thought of Clarissa. 'Can't talk over how revolting she is with *her*, now can I?'

'But you knew she was revolting before you married, you knew that, I knew that, the whole of London knew that, what can be so different now?'

'Now, now I'm in the same house as her, before, before I wasn't in the same house as her. I could just see her for a short time, and then go to the club and recover. Now, now she's everywhere, she's in the room, and even when she's not in the room, she's in my head, even when I'm alone. Tell you, sometimes I think she's even got into my head. Last night, in the middle of the night, do you know what I found myself doing? I found myself getting out of bed, kneeling beside the bed, and praying to die? I tell you I prayed to die, and I prayed that she might live forever, so that she wouldn't follow me. Every minute with her is Double Latin, and every hour Common Entrance.'

'She's certainly common,' agreed the Countess, and then returning to the point in question, 'but that too you knew before you married her.'

'It's different now.'

For a second the Countess looked at him with something near to pity. She knew, all too well, how 'different' life was once one person married another person, for she had known utter tedium in her first marriage, and genuine excitement in her second. She knew how the sound of someone's dull little habits, even at a distance, could be moquette to the soul, and how long the minutes seem between cocktail hour and dinner time if there is nothing to talk about, and how the night holds only an infinity of boredom and stale thoughts until at last morning comes, and the dull little habits start all over again.

But pity was fleeting, and she stopped short of feeling sorry for Andrew for more than a few seconds, for he had brought the wretched marriage upon himself, and if it was now all a horrid mess, it was a mess brought about by his own excesses. If he had been able to control his gambling, or his drinking, or just generally control something, he could have probably made more of a go of the things that he did slightly well, like finding escorts for debs, or organising dinner parties for Americans in historic houses, and everything would have been if not all right, at least tolerable, which as everyone knew was the very best to be hoped for in the one-way system of life; but since he had not been able to control any one area sufficiently he had had to pay the price, which was Clarissa Parker-Jones, taken for worse, and wouldn't get any better. When the Countess had been young her mother had had the habit of saying, grim-faced, and more than frequently, that only a fool climbed into an apple-pie bed, and so now she would have liked to have said to Andrew that he was a fool, except in his case he had sewn up his own pyjamas, and placed the thorns and the prickles between his own sheets.

In fact the poor man had put off marrying Clarissa Parker-Jones for so long that his prevarication had become a source of admiration to all. First there had been the question of his affairs to sort out, financial not amorous, and then there had been the business of the sudden and very urgent need for him to escort a bunch of dowagers overland to Nepal, which happily took so long that even the Countess had started to have high hopes of his never returning. Unfortunately, possibly due to the general lack of appeal of both the dowagers and Andrew, the party returned entirely intact, except for the loss of their thermal underwear, which had been cheerfully bartered by the ladies in return for fun and games with the natives.

Naturally, for he was more than human, Andrew had harboured the forlorn hope that on his return the Secretary of the Royal and Ancient Temple Society would have found, to his relief, that his fiancée Clarissa had found another object for her affections. Such optimism turned out to be ill-placed, for in fact Clarissa Parker-Jones had waited as patiently as any woman will, who has her eyes securely fixed on social advancement. And so poor Gillott discovered that time and excuses do run out when there is a price to pay, and he had finally been forced to say 'I will' to Clarissa in a small private ceremony for a few close

23

friends. It was a hideous punishment for a life of careless dissipation, and no one was more aware of it than the Countess when she saw Clarissa treading up the aisle towards Andrew, dressed entirely in mottled beige swathes, all topped off with a lime-green hat with matching pom-poms.

Kenya, it now appeared, over comforting gins and tonics in the Countess's drawing room, was a nightmare, nothing but Clarissa; no papers, no radio, just the Mu-Mu Maiden and the drip-drip-drip of her endless banalities. After only a couple of days she had befriended a Mr and Mrs Drew from Walton-on-Thames, and had insisted that they all dined together every night, in answer to which Andrew had taken to his bed with a pretend-funny tummy, and only emerged briefly to pack his bags, and return to London.

There was a small silence that always follows the unburdening of feelings, which the Countess filled with a topping up of their drinks, and general tidying up of Andrew's ashtrays, and other small pieces of activity, which were always the preliminaries to her being firm, unsympathetic, and ruthless.

'Of course you can't leave her,' she said, having now searched her crocodile handbag for a cigarette, and fitted it into the top of her tortoiseshell cigarette holder.

'I've got to, don't you see? It's making me ill.'

Andrew's large figure, sprawled against her grey silk sofa, sagged in despair at her words. There was certainly enough of him to feel ill. For no reason the word 'sackbutt' came into the Countess's head. It had nothing to do with anything, but somehow 'sackbutt' was the only way to describe Andrew at this moment. Nothing to do with the word's actual meaning, but if asked, she would definitely describe him as a boring old 'sackbutt'.

'Look, I'm with you on this old boy,' she said softening her tones, and changing her attitude, 'but three weeks is too short. It makes a woman look a fool, and you look a cad. Sort of thing that gets into the gossip columns.'

'Don't care what I get into any more, so long as it's not Clarissa's bed,' Andrew whined.

'Don't remember you being so sensitive before?' said the Countess.

24

'Getting "fixed up" is different from marriage. You get fixed up on a weekend, you fix someone else up, chances are you're drunk when you get to bed, and can't remember anything the next morning, and the same goes for everyone else. Can't get drunk twenty-four hours a day, that's the bloody trouble with marriage, just can't get drunk all night and all day. I know, I've tried. Trouble is I keep drinking myself sober. You know how it is.'

The Countess knew. Drink quenched nothing, not pain, not boredom, not fear. For her and Freddie – when Freddie was alive – drink had meant champagne, claret, colour, sparkle, soft voices, late evenings. Now, for her alone, it was merely punctuation, sometimes energy, occasionally sleep.

'Tell you what, tell you what I should do if I were you,' the Countess removed her cigarette holder from between her thin lips and pronounced. 'You should go to the country. It's traditional. You go and live in the country, and Clarissa gets so bored, she leaves you.'

'I am not going to live in her house in Surrey,' said Andrew. 'Rather top myself.'

'In that case move. Tell the silly woman you can't take Surrey, won't take Surrey. Find another house somewhere proper, do it up, stick her in it, she gets bored, leaves you. You get half the property, go back to town, rejoin your club, eh voilà.'

Andrew looked across at the Countess. During the last nightmareish weeks, even in his deepest misery, he had had the feeling that all along the beastly woman would get him out of his crisis, principally because she'd got him into it in the first place, for it was she who had fixed him up with Mu-Mu Maiden. But her present plan was nothing short of ingenious. He'd forgotten that the new Marriage Act benefitted penniless husbands as well as wives, and if only Clarissa could be induced to leave him, he could not but be a happy man again. Spring was on its way, and in the air, and he suddenly felt it. He pushed himself up from the sofa, and beamed at the Countess.

'Champagne lunch on me,' he announced.

It was on Clarissa, and they both knew it, but nevertheless as they walked off into Knightsbridge neither of them had cause to be in anything but a celebratory mood. Andrew had arrived at just the right time to relieve the Countess's boredom, and in her turn she had given him a plan, something to think about, a mental wooden horse to build secretly behind Clarissa's back. Just the thought that his present existence need not be forever was a tonic. And moving occupied a woman, it made her busy, it got her away from a man, so she went about prattling about infernal wallpapers, and other inanities. And then, given just one winter in the country, there was no doubt about it, Clarissa would go out of her mind and flee back to town leaving him in deep regret in their country house.

'It is with deep regret that Andrew Gillott has to announce that he and his wife are separating due to irreconcilable differences.' He could see it in the *Daily Mail*, at around about page fifteen. In the past he had often had cause, along with the rest of the world, to wonder when he saw 'irreconcilable differences' written, what that phrase exactly shielded? Perhaps some unspeakable practice of a physical nature, or extreme reluctance in some other area that the partners had not discovered until the knot of marriage had bound them in such a way that only the stroke of a legal hatchet could set them free; but now he knew that it could be nothing more sensational than the fact that she wore purple mu-mus, or talked about the weather when a chap was watching the racing, or refused to let him smoke in the bathroom; those were the 'sensational details' that so often lurked beneath 'irreconcilable differences'. Little dullnesses that the world would be only too pleased to mock, only to return to truffling for more sensational items in other people's lives.

In the restaurant Andrew raised his glass to the Countess. 'To an uncontested suit,' he said, and they both laughed, their eyes swivelling eagerly to the chef's recommendation for the day.

It was about the same time as her aunt was lunching with Andrew Gillot that Georgiana Longborough was sitting on a stool at the Harrods health food bar, and contemplating the top of a pineapple. Her slender legs were crossed elegantly in front of her, and she sat very upright, as a person will who has spent her childhood having her deportment corrected with the aid of large leatherbound books, which would be placed upon her head while she walked in a straight line. She wore a new navy-blue jacket with a stiff white piqué collar, and small brass buttons which ran to the side. The matching skirt was elegantly cut with a pleat at the front which presented her legs to great advantage, as did her high-heeled shoes. She was not dressed to not attract attention, and as she leant her left hand on the counter and picked up a piece of heavy cream paper, her dark hair swung forward, as it was meant to, and if someone had been sitting next to her they could have caught a little flavour of the 'Eau de Metal' scent that she wore. As it was there was no one next to her, and although her piece of paper was clearly printed in black ink across the top 'London', and again, appropriately, 'Harrods', and had such mildly exciting items as 'silk pyjamas', and 'lace pillowcases' written on it, she was filled with an inexpressible emptiness, and not even the vaguely peppery taste of the health juice gave her any kick. She was definitely not bored, for she knew what boredom felt like. Boredom was sitting next to someone dull at a dinner party, it was just missing a taxi, and not making the plane. It was six o'clock on a Sunday evening, and quarter past ten on a Monday. It was having to take Nanny her cocoa, and not being able to get into the film you wanted to see, and the feelings that you felt then, they were not the feelings that she felt at the present moment. They were positive 'if only' feelings, this feeling that she had now, that she had had for a few weeks now, this was a feeling of being utterly futile, in the way that a crinoline doll to cover a telephone was futile, it served no purpose. She served no purpose and what was worse she could not find a purpose to serve.

She had invitations, of course. Upon the chimneypiece of her London flat lay invitations to art galleries, to charity events, to weddings – at least two weddings – and her diary was, it appeared, full of people who were eager to invite her to dinner, or for the weekend, where she could be guaranteed to be decorative, occasionally amusing, but always perfectly able to fit in, for that was Georgiana's quality. She was able to fit in gracefully anywhere, and therefore people were prepared to invite her, knowing that she would not embarrass anyone. In her own mind, that was the very quality in herself that she most despised. At twenty-one she was unembarrassing to the point of dullness. She did not make passes at other people's husbands, she did not try to steal other people's lovers, (something which was 'de rigeur' with most of her friends) and she did not indulge in amusing incidents of the sort that give the Upper Class a bad name. Since her first affair at nineteen there had been no gossip column items written around her exploits. She had no desire to steal road signs, nor to embarrass anyone in any way, and it would seem, outwardly, that having taken a famous man as a lover when she was nineteen, she was now content to tread the safe social path for which her background and her looks made her suitable. But, although she was the heiress to a large house in the country and a small legacy provided her with enough income to look elegant and list such items as 'silk pyjamas' as necessities, she was not happy. Useless to point out poverty and unemployment to her, as useless as Nanny lecturing the reluctant eater to 'finish up' because of all the starving Chinese children. It was precisely because she had everything, and still felt futile, that she felt so empty.

There was good reason to suppose that she might have taken at least one lover since her first affair, but she had not. Her first lover, Kaminski, had been famous, sexually experienced and talented, and therein lay her problem, for she was quite unable to swop a Steinway Grand for a pub upright, and consequently had become, in the succeeding two years, a fashionable adornment, unattached and unable to attach. Not that she had not, occasionally, met other men who were mature, famous, rich and talented, but none of them had been as famous as Kaminski, none of them as rich, and none of them as incomprehensible to her. For, added to her ability to fit in, Georgiana had one more virtue, of which she was readily aware, she knew she was not clever. Kaminski had been clever. He had not bothered to talk to her a great deal about the subjects that interested him, for conversation had not played a part in their relationship, but she had heard him talk to other people, endlessly; and just as someone who stands in front of a great painting knows that it is great without knowing why it is, Georgiana knew that Kaminski was a great man, without knowing why he was. And in that too lay a hidden catch, for she was not the only person who knew that she had been the mistress of a great man; other men, initially all too interested in her, would come to know of it, and would then hold back from the comparison that they sensed might embrace them should they become involved with her. Kaminski as a lover had left her an emotional widow, and sometimes she felt that this would always be so.

She had fantasies, although she did not call them fantasies. Since they were based on the paperbacks that she bought once or twice a week, in the afternoons, her fantasies were remarkably unoriginal, but fleetingly satisfying. She would dream that she met someone in a lift, and that she knew instantly that he and she were fated. Or that she hired a car and the chauffeur turned out to be someone exciting, or that she was in a restaurant, and was introduced not, as was usual, to someone as dull as the person she was inevitably with, but to someone of Kaminski's stature, or at least someone of his electricity, and she would, once again, be an inspiration to someone intensely exciting. These little daydreams, as she thought of them, sustained her, and became an almost pathetic 'force motif' for her immaculate appearance, and for her ability to accept invitations despite the certain knowledge that what lay ahead would merely be a repetition of what lay behind her. Silk pyjamas, lace pillowcases, they were all part of an optimism that she did not feel.

Of course there was too the question of taste. She was by nature fastidious. It was not just the fact that Kaminski had been her first real lover, it was also that she was reluctant to take a lover as a prop, as other girls that she knew did. She was both too proud to stoop to such an instant remedy, preferring her loneliness, and too arrogant. Pride told her that it was not necessary, arrogance told her that it was not necessary for her. Lady Georgiana Longborough was special, so special, to herself anyway, that she would not take a shortcut, least of all for appearances. And so night after night, weekend after weekend, she would drive herself home to Longborough alone, or catch the train in solitude, until, as had happened recently, she resented anyone else accompanying her.

Someone sat down next to her, so close that they must surely catch a whisper of her scent. She felt them staring at her. She turned.

'Georgiana. I thought it was you. Your hair *so* different. Last time I saw you you had a sort of plait effect into your neck. For your party. Such a *pity* about the weather, *could* have been so lovely, but there we are, it can never be relied on in Wiltshire, can it? Now, tell me, is it true that the couple in the Lodge at Longborough pay you a peppercorn rent as *well* as doing the gardening and the housework? Because if this is so, I must tell a chum of mine, because she has a house, vast like Longborough, vaster actually, and it would be so useful to her to really know about it, because she is *desperate* at the moment. Desperate. Of course it must be a great source of comfort to your poor parents to be so well looked after, because I mean they were in a bit of a pickle, weren't they? And I must say I think, no matter what they say, I think they're really very well off, at Longborough, considering. No really. I do.'

Georgiana looked at Diana Farley, and felt a little wave of nausea. Mrs Farley never bothered to hide her malice, just as she never bothered to change her dreary green quilted jacket and her silk scarf when she came to London. Her nose was pointed, and still pink from the weather outside, and she carried an umbrella with a mock ivory handle and a Harrods bag in a heavy plastic, which on second glance proved to be vaguely worn, but which she probably carried in order to give the impression that she had just bought something.

'Oh, are you off?'

She glanced quickly down at the list before Georgiana had time to pick it up.

'Silk pyjamas? But my dear, how glamorous.'

'A present,' said Georgiana quickly, 'for my mother.'

'Charming. I wish my children bought me silk pyjamas, my children only buy me saucepans.'

She was delaying Georgiana so that she could assess exactly what she was wearing, and pass it on to the girlfriend she was meeting at the juice bar. Her eyes travelled swiftly, and the price of everything that Georgiana had on sprang into her eyes. The suit, beautifully cut, three hundred pounds, the shoes not a penny under eighty, but together with the handbag, at least a hundred and fifty, and then the jewellery, the heavy gold bracelet, the rings, the earrings, no doubt all purchased by that film director she'd had an affair with, but nevertheless entirely covetable – why, the whole girl must be worth over fifteen hundred pounds, as she was. Maddening really, but then if one went to bed with a famous man one could obviously expect to be repaid handsomely. She only wished that her Caroline could have a brief fling with someone rich, instead of going out with a boring little quantity surveyor, but there you were, Lady Georgie, as she was known in the village, was quite a little goer.

'Goodbye.'

'Goodbye, my dear.'

Georgiana walked away. She no longer felt just futile, now, but futile and cheap. Mrs Farley was a friend of Georgiana's mother, they were both linked by the same deep interest, they both did the *Daily Telegraph* crossword. Georgiana knew that Mrs Farley would know more about Georgiana than Georgiana knew about herself; and no doubt prior to their accidental meeting today Mrs Farley would have been given graphic descriptions of how Georgiana had put Nanny and her parents through hell converting Longborough into apartments. She would have heard of the inconveniences suffered when Georgiana had friends for the weekend, because they parked their cars in front of their wing, with the result that her parents could not enjoy the view from the library when they were having their gin and tonic at lunchtime. She would know of the enormous amounts of money lavished needlessly on the main part of the house where Georgiana now lived and, worst of all, how Georgiana had ruined the garden planting shrubs that they personally disliked, and altering shapes of flower beds to suit some modish taste.

Georgiana did not like to admit that 'Mrs F' had disturbed her, but she knew she must have for she found that she no longer had any interest in buying a pair of silk pyjamas, she was now filled with a desire to buy a half-dozen pairs of silk pyjamas, and more lace pillowcases than she owned pillows, but first she thought she would try on some jewellery. A thick gold necklace, such as she did not own and perhaps, for maximum annoyance when she returned to Wiltshire at the weekends, a gold chain for her ankle.

Naturally the man behind the counter, who produced the

gold collar for her to look at, knew that she could afford it, which she could not. He knew it because he could recognise money and class at a few yards.

She held the thick gold collar against her suit. It was of the kind that the ancient Egyptian ladies wore. It felt strange to see herself in the looking-glass provided, solemn and alone, contemplating buying an item which instinctively both she and the assistant knew someone else should be buying for her. But, on the other hand, there was something slightly rakish about the situation, as if she had obtained money from some immoral source and was now enjoying the fruits of her decadence. The assistant stood behind her, and suggested that she should unbutton her tight white collar to reveal her throat. She did so, and then lifting up her hair a little she allowed him to fasten the necklace, and then she dropped her dark hair, and they both stared at her in the glass. The formality of the moment grew, until in both the assistant's mind, and in Georgiana's, it seemed as if he might be buying it for her.

'Beautiful,' said the assistant, meaning Georgiana.

'Beautiful,' Georgiana agreed, meaning the necklace.

They held the moment for some minutes, both reluctant to fracture the image in the glass, and return to the business of payment, but eventually the assistant unclasped the necklace, Georgiana dropped her hair, and the piece was laid in a long velvet box and posted into an envelope, which was placed in her now gloved hand.

'Thank you, madam,' the assistant said.

Georgiana looked at him, and smiled slightly. She was feeling better now. Mrs Farley, her malice, the village, her parents, what other people said about her, they were all retreating slightly now that she had bought something very expensive that she could not afford. But it was not enough, although she would set aside the gold ankle chain until another day, the silk pyjamas could not be left, any more than the pillowcases, or a pair of pale grey stockings with a tiny motif that she had seen advertised in *Harpers and Queen*. And so she took the lift to the first floor, and bought her pyjamas and her pillowcases, both made in Italy and very expensive, and then feeling almost satiated she descended to the ground floor and bought a new scent and the desired stockings.

In the taxi home, she sat back and looked at her own image in the driver's back, as she always did. She was beautiful, she was carrying a great many parcels, and because she was alone she was able to savour everything – the wet streets outside, the sway of the taxi, the change in the light as early evening moved in to take possession of the afternoon, even the reality of the cab interior with its hint of stale smoke and old newspaper, even that was pleasing, providing a coarse-grained edge to the luxury in her arms.

Her flat was really just a large room with a kitchen and bathroom off, decorated in an acceptable pale cream, and coloured by spring flowers brought from Longborough. There was no excess of china, no flower paintings and no lace curtains. It was a room where a man would not feel ill at ease. The furniture was comfortable rather than pretty, and the bed large, covered in brown velvet and an old fur coat that had once belonged to her grandmother. It had a great many cushions arranged upon it to encourage visitors to use it as a sofa.

Georgiana laid down her parcels and looked at them lovingly, then after a moment she went to the windows and, although it was still light she drew the curtains and lit a small lamp. She undressed slowly and decoratively, for in her mind someone was watching her, then opened the velvet box from Harrods; clasped her new gold necklace around her neck and lay down on the bed. The velvet was smooth and soft, and her body was so beautiful and so pale. She felt utterly content.

Still without her clothes, she later picked up a small leather-bound volume of Shakespeare's sonnets, and turning the pages of the old book she searched for some lines that she could memorise. She had great difficulty in understanding poetry, but she persisted in reading it, because in poetry, it seemed, love was spoken of in a beautiful way, and she liked to read about love, just as she liked to go to museums and look at paintings where love was depicted in rich and glowing colours recognisable to her in ways that the paperback novels that she bought were not.

'As easy might I from myself depart,
As from my soul which in thy breast doth lie.'

She repeated these lines aloud in a melodic if Upper Class tone, for she had not the vowel sharp voice of those whom the Countess was apt to describe as 'County creeps'.

Repeating beautiful lines, saying words which she could never imagine being able to invent, had a soothing effect upon her spirits, and from not being able to contemplate even the idea of going out, of disturbing her mystic contemplation of herself, she was now able to remember that she had been asked to a preview of some paintings and sculpture. Appropriately the sculpture was nude. Female nudes, in poses of which Nanny could never approve.

She dressed for her new necklace, in a heavy black satin blouse and stiff taffeta skirt. Because of this obligation to dress for her new acquisition, she knew she would be overdressed, but knowing this she immediately imagined to herself that she was going 'on' somewhere else. If anyone asked her she would name somewhere vague, and anonymous, for so long as wherever you were going on to was vague, people naturally assumed it was somewhere specific and famous, and modesty was forbidding further discussion.

The art gallery was near enough to take a taxi, so once more she sat in the back of a cab and contemplated her own immaculate image, and then eventually when even that tired as an occupation, she opened the preview catalogue. Without much interest she read that the artist had been born in Brentford, educated at a comprehensive and afterwards at the Slade School of Art, following which he had spent some time working in France and Italy. He had had two previous exhibitions, one in Manchester and another in Glasgow.

The taxi stopped. Georgiana shut the catalogue, and as she climbed decoratively from the taxi she wondered why she was attending Augustus Hackett's preview, and knew the reply without forming the words in her minds. She was bored.

She supposed she must know the owner of the gallery, since he made a point of kissing her, but she had the feeling that it was probably because he was kissing most of the new arrivals as a matter of form. She declined a glass of wine as everyone well-versed in previews must, and approached the first piece of sculpture entitled 'Sunday Afternoon'. Quite obviously Mr Hackett was not in the habit of spending his weekends gardening and taking tea on the lawn, for 'Sunday Afternoon' was most erotic. So erotic that Georgiana felt that the time that she spent in contemplating it should be finely judged. Too long spent in looking at it might seem salacious, and too short a little bourgeois. She counted to fifty, and then moved on. She was not alone. A man followed her. She knew from the photograph on the back of the catalogue that it was Augustus Hackett, Esq., not yet R.A.

She hoped that she could continue to ignore him, but her ability to ignore someone who was staring at her quite openly, almost rudely, was limited.

'What do you think?'

Georgiana hesitated. She didn't feel it was quite right for the artist to approach you at a preview, yet she didn't know why it was that she felt that, but it was as if the bride or groom at a wedding was following you around, instead of standing still in the receiving line. She tried to think of an appropriate word to use for 'Sunday Afternoon', and as always happened when she was expected to supply just the right adjective, her mind became quite empty. She would have liked to have said 'it's very nice', but she knew that 'nice' would not be acceptable, for Miss Gingle, her English teacher at Grantley Abbey, had always poured scorn on 'nice'. It was not an adjective that could be used about 'Sunday Afternoon' anyway, because whatever was happening between the couple depicted was certainly not 'nice'. 'Sexy' would be cheap, 'fascinating' should only be applied to hats, and 'irresistible' to dresses and puddings, and so she was left with 'brilliant'.

For a moment the carefully tough manner slipped as the artist looked, with gaze softened, on his work. He obviously agreed with her, so that was all right.

'No, it's not bad, is it?' he said in the real tones upon which Brentford had left their mark.

Georgiana started to move, feeling that she had now said all that could be required, and that there was an end to the matter.

'Not buying then?'

He was following her now.

'I'm sorry?'

'There's no need to be – look, I'll be truthful. I really fancy you, so if you give me your name and address, I'll let you have "Sunday Afternoon". A gift from the artist. Now how about that for a bargain?'

Georgiana started to say, 'Don't be silly.'

'No, really.'

He put both hands on the wall either side of her, so that she was trapped.

'Please –'

'For Christ's sake, what a bargain. That's extremely expensive.'

He nodded towards the sculpture, but kept his hands either side of her on the wall.

'So am I.'

He started to laugh.

'Come on.'

'But I don't want "Sunday Afternoon", that is, I've nowhere to put it,' she lied, thinking that it was only really suitable for the kitchen garden, where it might be improved with some chives or chervil growing round it.

'It's not bronze, it's fibreglass, not even your address is worth a bronze, Miss –'

He leant forward to catch her name, and Georgiana heard herself saying 'Not Miss –'

'Mrs?'

Gus looked at her surprised. She didn't seem married. Beautiful, self-assured, rich, but not married. Having already fancied her, he now fancied her like mad. The aloof manner, the husband doubtless waiting to dine with her.

'Not Mrs either,' said Georgiana, mischievously. 'Now I really must go.'

'But you haven't seen the rest of the exhibition –'

'No, really, I must. It's my husband. He's waiting for me.'

Gus took one of her hands and kissed it. And then he watched as she hailed a taxi, and climbed in, her shapely legs, her mellifluous voice. He knew that he had to have her, whoever her husband was. He went back into the gallery and wrote down her address.

This time Georgiana was quite unable to look at her reflection in the cab driver's back, but stared out of the window.

At home alone she unwrapped a pair of her new silk pyjamas. She lay once more upon the velvet-covered bed, and picked up her little leather-bound book of Shakespeare's sonnets.

'As easy might I from myself depart,
As from my soul which in thy breast doth lie.'

Chapter Three

Patti looked round her dining room with a vague sense of terror. The batons had been placed preparatory to the material that Fulton had chosen on her behalf being put on the walls. She was not sure that a mixture of yellow and orange was going to be exactly right for Gerard and her. She was not sure she liked orange with yellow, nor was she sure that Gerard would like it, any more than the really rather old furniture that Fulton had chosen to go with it; but not being sure was not a good reason, it seemed, for not having any of these items, for as Gerard kept saying, 'There's no point in keeping a dog and doing the barking yourself.' Although Patti was not absolutely sure what he meant by this, nevertheless she imagined it had everything to do with saying 'yes' rather than 'no' to whatever Fulton proposed.

Of course it would be much simpler if she had lived in the country before, but she had not, and she was only now getting used to the funny stares that she received when she went into the village in her black leather jodhpurs. The fact that Gerard wore baggy old jodhpurs was one thing, but the fact that she wore new leather ones – straight from the Kings Road, mind – was, it appeared, quite another.

'It's because you don't ride,' Gerard had said to her yesterday, but she really couldn't see what he meant.

There were aspects about the country that she was growing to like. For instance, she liked the fact that her garden was walled, and she was looking forward to the hot summer days when she could wander about without anything on, for there had never been enough room for wandering on her top floor balcony in Putney.

And she liked the view from her bedroom window of the lawn, and the old yew tree, and she thought once summer came that it would be fun to pick an apple off one of the fruit trees in the orchard, even though Gerard had told her that they were neglected, and the fruit was maggoty, even so, it was something that she had promised herself that she would do. Of course she missed the shops dreadfully, but she had found a quick way to Bath, and an even quicker way to the station and the commuter train to London, so that she knew that she was still in touch with the things that really meant more to her, or at least as much, as horses and the country meant to Gerard. Really, it was only her great love for Gerard that had brought her to this place, for she would never have chosen it for herself, on her own; in fact it was the last place in the world that she would live on her own. Nevertheless, since she was here, and since Knightey was with her, she was quite enjoying it.

The people who lived around were, it was true, just a little buttoned up, but once the house was finished she meant to give a party and ask them all back, champagne and the lot, but until then she had to wrestle with the problem of getting the house finished, of lying awake at night and staring at the ceiling, and wondering whether or not to tent it as well as the dining room, of really thinking about whether to go for tangerine satin in the guest room, or to risk cream with no colour to relieve it whatsoever?

'Apricot could work, with little rosettes and tassels everywhere. It could work,' Fulton had said, his mouth pursing into what Gerard vulgarly described as a 'horse's bottom'. 'It could work.'

'But will it?' Patti had asked.

'That's for you to decide,' Fulton had replied, before sashaying off to inspect a really rather lovely Regency commode that he had found at auction, and managed to snatch from under the horrible nose of one of his rivals.

Frankly, as he had said to Elliott only last night, it was all very well 'advising' Patti, but you could only advise so much – something in the house had to be her, it couldn't all be him.

Maybe the 'her' bit would be the guest room (except tangerine satin made him feel quite sick). Or maybe he would have to give in over the gold taps shaped into swans' heads with onyx shower attachment? Or maybe it would have to be the *telephone*, for heaven's sake, which was made by Boudoir Fones and shaped like a woman's hand with mock emeralds in the hand piece, or whatever you called it. Whatever he allowed her, he would definitely have to allow her *one* thing, and deciding on that one thing gave him the most crashing headache. Still, even so, he had to admit that 'Lady Tizzy', as they had nicknamed Patti, had afforded them so much amusement over the past few weeks that although the job was not going to be one that you could boast about to your friends – *the stories*.

'My dear,' said Elliott to the Countess when she telephoned, 'I don't know what we should have done for giggles without "Lady Tizzy". Really. It's been a laugh a minute.'

'Mary's back in London – Capri was tiresome,' said the Countess, who only used the telephone to say what *she* had to say.

'Really. Frightfully well, is she?' asked Elliot, staring with some satisfaction at one of his fingernails which was quite gloriously pink and healthy, with a very large moon waning at the bottom.

'No, far from it,' said the Countess with satisfaction, 'she and Luscious have been having a horrid time out there. His book, you know that boring little book he wrote called *The Bay Tree*? Well it did dreadfully, and now he has turned to poetry without commas.'

'So they're back, are they?'

Elliott made a little moué at the telephone receiver as he said 'so they're back', and he thought 'let's hope for their sake they don't stay in London very long.' He liked the Countess's daughter.

'Yes, they're back,' said the Countess. 'She looks older, of course. And he's broken a tooth.'

'Charming,' said Elliott.

'They're determined on buying a house somewhere in Wiltshire, so no doubt they'll be imposing themselves.'

'I don't mind,' said Elliott, adding silently 'so long as they don't bring you'.

'Frankie. You know Lavinia's Frankie?'

Alas Elliott did, only too well, he was a boring man, rude and boring, who reminded Elliott of the worst excesses of heterosexuality, as he was constantly referring to his various bits and parts in a loud foreign way. He, Frankie, was one of the many reasons that Elliott had decided to distance himself from London, and 'that set', as he referred to the Countess's friends.

'Frankie thinks she's tiring of him,' said the Countess.

Of course *she* would have to tire of *him*, it would be quite unheard of for *him* to tire of *her*. It was definitely not on for a man to tire of Lavinia, no, she would have to do the tiring. Pom, pom, tiddley pom.

'Luscious', as the Countess referred to 'Lucius', was Lady Mary's lover, and an American writer who 'aspired'. The Countess could not approve of writers, least of all American writers. She approved of books, she approved of furniture, but she did not approve of the people who wrote the books or made the furniture. She would not have dined with Sheraton. On the other hand she had been known to approve of various members of her, or other people's, staff, or 'servants' as they used to be known. If a gardener was good at his job, if a cook was an artist at her work, they were allowed to cheek the Countess, because this meant that they were 'characters', and that was perfectly all right. People who looked after other people's needs, provided that they were brilliant at it, were allowed a lot of licence, and you could quote them with a little giggle afterwards, in the vein of 'Do you know what Beamington said to me last night?' That was perfectly all right, but 'Luscious' was not. He penned silly novels, and if you didn't know he wasn't, you'd have sworn he was a confirmed bachelor when you met him.

'I think I can hear a customer arriving,' said Elliott suddenly, for he could only take so much of the Countess's malice, and then suddenly it made him feel horribly anxious about what she would be saying about him when she put the telephone down and dialled someone else. 'Yes, yes, it is, it's a customer.'

'I can't hear the shop bell,' said the Countess.

'You wouldn't, it's broken,' said Elliott, lying and crossing his fingers at the same time, so that God would know that he didn't mean it.

'I too must wend,' said the Countess, and she quickly put

down the receiver without saying goodbye, which she knew would upset Elliott.

It didn't upset Elliott in the least. He merely went back to the serene contemplation of his fingernail. He was not going to let that old tabby upset him. In fact there had been a customer vaguely hovering outside the shop window, and there was one still. She had arrived in a chauffeur-driven Roller, and was now pushing the shop door open. Elliott rose to greet her. Sure to be either a demi-lune or a commode by the looks of her.

'I'm not lying around like a French poodle in tangerine satin,' said Sir Gerard loudly.

Patti closed her eyes, and then opened them again quickly, because a piece of her thick black mascara had broken off, and was now firmly lodged in a corner of her left eye.

'Oh very well, baby darling, whatever you say. Shall I just leave it to Fulton, then?'

'Baby darling' opened a bottle of tonic, and poured it with dextrous brevity over his large gin. He liked his horse, he liked the country, he might even get to like the house, he just could not get to like this orgy of decorating. To his mind, as to the mind of most men of any distinction or taste, a house had to have three things for comfort. A large fireplace for log fires, a place for the drink, and a boot room where you could whack in and remove your hunting boots. Otherwise everything else was just 'fol de rol'. Perhaps he'd been through it too many times? Perhaps all too often and anon he had heard persons, female persons, carrying on about peach and nectarine, or whatever, and now the feelings of inglorious déjà vu that such conversations brought on panicked him. He chucked his first gin back, and then started out towards the drinks table for his second. The trouble with girls like Patti was that they had no brains. It was very possible that having no brains made them concentrate more, and to a greater degree and at an earlier age, on the things for which men would seek them, and not on the things for which men would not seek them. Certainly he had not decided to spend his declining years with Patti because of her reading list, for it would have proved a pretty blank experience. Nor indeed for her grasp of such subjects as eighteenth-century French politics, or folklore among the hop pickers of Kent, or even elementary dressage, but he had hoped to discuss something other than 'tenting' in the latter part of the twentieth century, and the rival merits of peach or cream satin. He had to think of a delicate way of conveying this to her.

'Patti darling?'

'Yes, baby darling?'

'Shut up.'

'What's that, baby darling?'

'I said "shut up". About the tenting, just shut up. Can't take another minute of it.'

Patti went to the mantelpiece and picked up her packet of Marlboro cigarettes, and her very last set of book matches from Mark's Club, which suddenly seemed to be part of a life that she would never see again, and which she equally felt she might like to go back to. She didn't know anything about 'decor' or the country, or anything really, and now Knightey was getting cross about it and making her feel as if she might need to sit down and have a Valium sandwich. In London, in London everything had been all right, and she had known where she was at; now, here, she was in a pickle, and even Knightey was cross, which he nearly never ever was. She would not utter one more word about anything of it any more to Gerard, not to anyone, except Fulton. She would just let Fulton get on with it. She went to the kitchen. Tonight she was cooking a nice tinned soup, followed by a frozen lasagne with salad. At least here she was at home, at least she did know how to cook.

Mrs Dupont had never been further than the hall of the Hall, so when she received a telephone call to the effect that the Marchioness of Pemberton wished her to come up and take coffee with her, in her private sitting room, she looked forward to it with the same sense of intense excitement that someone might feel when receiving an invitation to an investiture at Buckingham Palace. This was indeed a turn-up for the books, she thought, as she tried to decide on the most suitable skirt for taking coffee with a Marchioness, albeit informally. She settled on a kilted affair with a pair of navy-blue tights, and her good walking shoes from Church's in Knightsbridge. Sensible but good, that was the image she wished to convey, together with a manner that would be both interested and interesting, which must mean that her future relationship with the Marchioness would be elevated to something closer than the little dollops of condescension that she had been handed at infrequent intervals before.

Of course she knew, or rather she suspected, that something just a little dramatic must have happened to the Marchioness for her to raise the telephone and ask someone such as herself for coffee. Normally this could never be, for they were not just worlds apart, but universes apart, as most ordinary people must be from a woman whose husband owned five houses, seven cars, fifteen racehorses, and a private art collection.

No, something must have happened to the Marchioness, something to do with the village, that had motivated her to invite Mrs Dupont for coffee. Naturally Mrs Dupont had not told Margaret Paine, that would never do. Principally because she did not trust Margaret not to lift the telephone and get herself invited too. That could happen, it had not been unknown for her to push herself in some direction or the other quite shamelessly, if she thought she was missing out on something. No, Margaret would know nothing of Mrs Dupont's coffee morning until it had been over for at least a day.

'It's Lady Tisbury,' said the Marchioness.

She sat behind a Georgian coffee pot, a Georgian cream jug, and two bowls of sugar, one brown and one white, the whole arranged on a wooden tray with handles that the butler had placed before her only minutes before. Mrs Dupont breathed in the millions that were backing up this matinal scene. How simple money made everything! Clean sparkling old china, clean sparkling old silver, even the air seemed to have been polished by unseen hands.

'Yes, Lady Tisbury,' said the Marchioness again, having waited for Bloss to withdraw. 'Do you know her?'

Mrs Dupont experienced a small sense of disappointment. She had discussed Lady Tisbury endlessly, at bridge, at the village shop, even in the garage when she was having her Mini Traveller filled up, and she didn't really want her visit to the Hall to be a mere reproduction of all her previous conversations, which were only mere reproductions of all the others that she knew everyone else was having.

'Yes, I know Lady Tisbury, Lady Pemberton, in that I've met her, and I've talked to her, but I don't know her as a chum, if that's what you mean? No, I don't.'

Judging from the Marchioness's expression it was just as well that she didn't, she quickly realised, for the Marchioness's face became suddenly a little contorted, even twisted you could say, and she had hardly handed Mrs Dupont her cup of coffee (too full alas to be able to turn it over and make out whether it was Wedgewood or not) than she gave a little gasp – there was no other word for it.

'I'm most relieved to hear you say so,' said Lady Pemberton, 'most relieved. Isn't she quite frightful?'

'Frightful.'

'Quite frightful. My dear, I didn't know where to look when she came here, I ended up staring at my feet.'

Now she stared at Mrs Dupont. Mrs Dupont stared back. She couldn't help it. Lady Pemberton had never called her 'my dear' before. It was a first.

'If, Mrs Dupont, if I had known what she was like, well, frankly that would have been it. I mean it. I could not have invited her, but no one told me, not one person told me, and you can imagine Lord Pemberton, well, no you can't – he had a FIT.'

Mrs Dupont lowered her voice to a deeply reverential tone before she said, 'I can imagine.'

'Now tell me, you must, what do you know about her? She was a Bluebell Girl, wasn't she?'

Mrs Dupont had not known that Lady Tisbury was a Bluebell Girl but, now that she did, she was most happy to receive that information, as would be the bridge party tonight, the village shop tomorrow and the garage next week. She would have liked to have said that she was not surprised, but she did not, because it would be better to find out first how Lady Pemberton knew of this.

'Of course I had heard,' she said, immediately assuming the expression of someone who having heard would never have dreamed of repeating it until that moment.

'Oh, so you *had*?' said Lady Pemberton, and she stared intensely at the view behind Mrs Dupont's head. 'Of course it accounts for everything. The way she dresses, the manner, everything can be accounted for once you know that about her, can't it? I saw a programme on the television once, and it had something about the Bluebells on it, and they were not – how shall I say it? – the Bluebells were not country women. She'll never fit it in, will she?'

Lady Pemberton's gaze reverted to Mrs Dupont's face, and Jane Dupont knew at once that she was being told something that was going to be of interest about future village policy towards Lady Tisbury.

'Of course it takes everyone to make up village life, you, me, the vicar, and naturally Lady Tisbury, now she's here, but somehow I do wonder whether she'll fit in, don't you?'

Mrs Dupont, quite naturally, did wonder. She also wondered just how much that magnificent diamond on Lady Pemberton's finger was insured for? 'Hardly Woolworth's' as she remarked to Margaret Paine later, for oddly enough she found it was quite impossible to pass the Paines' front door as she drove home, and not call in and tell them of her morning at the Hall, and of all that Lady Pemberton had told her.

In fact Jennifer had not told her very much. All she had done was to warn Mrs Dupont, which was only proper, for the fact that Lady Tisbury was titled might well have led persons such as she to be taken in by her, to think that she was acceptable, and that could lead to many confusions. No, she felt that she had done absolutely the right thing in speaking to Mrs Dupont as she had, but nevertheless, as she watched Mrs Dupont's decrepit little motor car departing down the long drive, Jennifer was left with a feeling that she had not done the right thing, even though she knew that she had. She had not done the wrong thing, of course, but on the other hand, she might not have done the right thing, in the sense that gossiping to someone in the village might well be the wrong thing, even if what one was telling them was the right thing.

She debated with herself so intensely on this exact point of conscience, that had not the telephone rung and interrupted her thoughts she feared she might have developed a headache as a result. Nevertheless she let it ring a while, for she always thought that living in the country as she did, it sounded a little over-eager if one answered it straight away, or worse still rushed in breathless from the garden in order to answer it. The very fact that the sound of the telephone came as such a terrific relief when one lived in the Shires was reason enough not to let the rest of the world know.

As soon as she picked it up, she deeply regretted that she had not left it ringing and ringing, and never answered it at all, for it was her mother. Newly married, so pleased with herself and so full of news that Jennifer automatically reached into her desk drawer and took out an Altoid indigestion tablet. No words could describe the acid that welled up inside her when she heard the new Mrs Andrew Gillott purring on the other end of Mr Bell's personal invention. Mrs Gillott had had a perfectly incredible honeymoon, naturally. She had a perfect tan, naturally, but more than that she had the most perfectly wonderful news. For one ghastly moment Jennifer wondered whether her mother could be pregnant? Bad enough surely to have to go to her wedding and now endure her falsely coquettish post-honeymoon airs, but the thought that she might be big with something other than sheer complacency was so fearful that Jennifer found herself cramming yet another Altoid into her mouth.

'We have decided to buy a country house near you,' said the ex-Mrs Parker-Jones, now fully fledged on a proper social course as 'the Hon. Mrs Andrew Gillott'. Something which she took pleasure in writing out many times when she was quite on her own.

'Near us where?' snapped Jennifer.

The new Mrs Gillott stared at the receiver. Jennifer did not sound at all herself, not at all. It was not at all like Jennifer to snap.

'Near you where what?' she asked.

'Near us where in the country? In Norfolk? In the Lake District? In Wiltshire? Where?'

Enough was quite enough, and Jennifer having endured nothing but the horridest time from her mother was now quite determined that the fact that she owned more property and took precedence over her would not go unnoticed, no matter what her mother felt.

'Near you in Wiltshire, of course,' said Clarissa, 'where else could it be?'

Jennifer knew that her mother loved to ignore her precedence and her property, and even the fact that Jennifer was actually younger than Clarissa was never referred to in anything but the direst times, as when it was necessary to point out that Jennifer was not conducting herself as she should.

When she had first moved into the Hall her mother had found it quite, quite impossible to come and visit her there. This was because the hideous sight of Jennifer's glorious new home, her paintings, her silver and her butler were all too much for her. She gave many and various reasons for her inability to visit. Sometimes it was because the memory of Jennifer's dear father was too much for her. What would he not have done to have seen her so happily settled? Here it seemed that Jennifer did not share the same memory of her father, for happy as she was sure that he would have been at the sight of so much wealth, it would nevertheless, she knew, have given rise to grave doubts within him. He had not approved of aristocrats. They were unstable. They came by fortunes and wealth without any achievement, and as a result they did not know how to husband their assets, let alone their wives. They did not have a genuine regard for money that a City man such as himself had, only a fascination with what it could buy.

'No feeling for investment,' he would say shaking his head dubiously, before folding his newspaper to a perfect shape, and putting it under his arm.

He would not have approved of Pember, but neither would he have disapproved of him, and whenever Jennifer thought of the meeting that might have taken place as a result of her desire to marry Pember she was awfully glad that her father had died before she had become the Seventh Marchioness of Pemberton. Not that an inability to absolutely approve would have been only on one side. It would not have. It would have been on both sides, for nowadays she could never ever see Pember passing more than five minutes in company with someone such as her father, without his eyes beginning to shut, almost openly. So although she was very sorry her father had died, at the time, nevertheless she was very glad that if he had had to go, he had gone when he did, for it had saved them all a great deal of embarrassment.

'House hunting near us in Wiltshire? Well, then we must keep an eye open for you,' said Jennifer, who had no intention of doing any such thing.

What a relief it was to live in the middle of a large estate, for it meant that wherever the new Mrs Gillott decided to live would be acres away from her daughter, even should she take up residence at the Gate Lodge, which heaven forfend.

'We shall probably be down during the week when we hear of a property,' Mrs Gillott announced into the telephone. 'By the way, guess whom I saw the other day?'

Jennifer knew her mother would never ask her that question if she thought that her daughter had the answer to it. Nevertheless it would be a great moment of small triumph if she could come up with the right name, which of course she couldn't. Instead Jennifer bit into her Altoid tablet, and crunched it noisily.

'Lady Mary. Remember her from your season? Georgiana Longborough's cousin? She's back in London. I must say she does look a little older.'

'Probably because she is,' said Jennifer, and then she said, 'Oh dear, Bloss has just come in.'

A constant reference to Bloss was one of the few things that could make her mother put the telephone down, for they both knew that although Clarissa was an Honourable now, and although she had a little money, she would never in a thousand years be able to afford a butler, and it gave her great discomfort to be reminded of this. Jennifer replaced the receiver, and found herself hoping that it would be Clarissa's turn to reach into a drawer and find an Altoid tablet.

She picked up her sewing, and glanced at the clock. It would be fully fifteen minutes until Nanny came back with Charles from his walk, and during that time she thought she would sew a little of the bargello cushion that she was making and think about Lady Mary. She just couldn't image the tall, willowy, beautiful Lady Mary as looking 'older', but since her mother was one of those people who could spot a pound of flesh added from a hundred yards, or a wrinkle that had not been there before, or heart disease, or pregnancy, it was hard not to believe her. It was also not displeasing to think about.

She would like to telephone Georgiana, for she was after all Lady Mary's cousin, but Georgiana was not in her world any more, as girls never are when one of them is married and the other is not.

Perhaps she could hint to Pember that she would like to ask a few people down? Or perhaps she could not, knowing Pember and his penchant for not socialising. Whichever way, she knew that sooner or later she had to see Lady Mary again for she was one of the heroines of Jennifer's life, and someone whom the dumpy young Jennifer had aspired to imitate. In fact, even now, if she was a little unsure of herself, she would imagine herself to be Lady Mary, and certainly there were various inflections and words that she always used, which she knew were inflections and words that Lady Mary used. 'Tolerable' was one, and 'decorative' was another. But to think of those words being used by someone who was no longer quite so decorative was intolerable.

Augustus Hackett had sent Georgiana flowers. It was only to be expected. They were tasteful early-summer flowers, pale pinks and whites. She had been sent flowers before, naturally, a great many flowers, but never by Kaminski. Kaminski had bought her clothes, not flowers, and he had dressed her in them, most carefully. He so loved to dress her that sometimes she thought that he had had an affair with her only to be allowed to dress her. He had liked to dress her not in the bedroom, but in the drawing room, starting from her stockings, and ending with shoes. She must always be very serious when he did this, which was difficult, for at nineteen solemnity was naturally hilarious. Once he had even slapped her for laughing, not on her face, for she could never have forgiven that, and he must have known it, but on her arm, so she had learnt that he meant her not to laugh. Perhaps because of this, because Kaminski had never bought her anything as mundane as flowers, Georgiana was not impressed by Mr Hackett's flowers. They were merely a perfectly proper tribute to her appeal. She put them on her davenport and went shopping.

She went to the General Trading Company where she bought some jars for the kitchen which had ingredients written on them in French, which she thought might make the contents seem more exciting. She would have liked to have bought more than just jars, but her thick gold necklace under her silk dress was a smooth reminder that she would have to sell a hideous piece of jade left to her by a godfather, before there was to be any more buying.

Naturally it was no coincidence that, having shopped, she should pass the art gallery wherein lay 'Sunday Afternoon', and a post-preview Augustus Hackett. She knew he would be there, and that if she stood on the other side of the glass outside that he would see her.

'Lady Longborough.'

She remembered now, just in time, that she was supposed to be married.

'You got my flowers?'

'No,' she lied, and then regretted it, because he looked crestfallen.

'I sent you some flowers, this morning, they should have been delivered by now.'

'Really?'

'Yes, really.'

He looked at her, and suddenly what Kaminski used to call 'le rouge regard' passed between them.

'Give us a break, my lady,' he mocked.

'I don't know what you mean?'

He took one of her hands and kissed it. Obviously a habit of his. His own hands were long-fingered with funny square-shaped nails, and dark hair on the back. They made her shiver, probably because she knew from looking at them that he must be good with women. He knew what they were like. Kaminski used to say that women's bodies meant more to them than their minds, no matter what they tried to tell you.

'You'll come to lunch then,' he said, ruling out the question mark quite pointedly.

Georgiana found herself hoping that the lunch would be a

disaster, that they would sit opposite each other and find nothing whatsoever to say, and that he would be gauche, and that he would talk about things that bored her, for she bored quite easily; but unfortunately for her sense of what was fitting none of these things happened, and if there were occasional silences it was only because they were filled with that inexplicable urgency to make love which can happen between two people who have not passed more than an hour in each other's company, and are hardly aware of even each other's Christian names.

Of course she did not have to go to his studio, and run up the stairs with him, and start to make love, she did not have to do it, because she was a person who, in part of her mind, was reasonable, but in another way she did have to do it, because she knew that if she didn't do something soon, she would never do anything, and Kaminski would always be written indelibly on those private areas that only he had, as yet, discovered.

And so when it became quite clear that calling him, somewhat self-consciously, 'Gus' was not the greatest intimacy that he wished to achieve with her, she did follow him up his studio stairs, wondering at the sculptures that crowded each step, the old red curtain that hung in front of the door, and then the immense room in which he lived and worked. She undressed with now practised artistry, until she stood in only her thick gold necklace. And he, forgetting his bravura from the night before, his self-boast of easy conquest, found only that he throbbed with that particular excitement which a man experiences when faced with making love to a beautiful girl on an early afternoon in spring.

Chapter Four

Fulton was furious because Elliott, who normally always elected to stay in charge of the shop, was out. It seemed that he had been invited by the Marchioness of P. to look at her library with a view to redecorating it. It was just a little maddening, Fulton had to admit, since he himself was still stuck at Flint House with the tenting. Even so, it wasn't so maddening that it would cause a rift, and it meant that Elliott could ask the Pembertons to lunch with Lady Mary and Lucius, and they would all be able to have a jolly.

He glanced at the long-case clock in the hall. Elliott should be home soon, and Fulton would learn all no doubt about her ladyship, of whom it was said that she had the taste of a publican's wife, all red flock, glazed chintz, and masses of stiff little rose beds in all the wrong places. At least poor Lady Tizzy, at least she *knew* that she didn't have any taste, and left it all to him.

To while away the time until Elliott's return Fulton wrote out Sunday's menu in his special menu writing, italic and black, with little Elizabethan swirls at the ends of words. He had, of course, planned the whole menu already. It would be quite mouth-watering in its delicacy. Fish mousse with a pale coral sauce, little noisettes of lamb with no herbs spared, followed by a crushed biscuit ice cream with raspberry sauce. He held the menu up. The luncheon was going to be so pink and perfect he felt like having a lie-down – talking of which, here was Elliott, pink, but not perfect, fresh from driving with the Volkswagen's hood down.

'*Well*?'

'*Well*.'

'Elliott, si tu ne raconte tout, toute de suite I'll never speakez to you again.'

'Lucky for some,' said Elliott, emptying his pockets of change, and putting it into the drawer of the hall table, a little habit of his that he always observed even if he went out and came back in again a dozen times a day.

Fulton wanted to scream, because Elliott was looking so important, positively plump with news, but there was nothing for it but to wait for him to pronounce, so instead of screaming he popped a cachou into his mouth and sucked on it a little too loudly.

'*Well*,' Elliott began again, 'she only wanted to paint the carvings in the library.'

'So what did you *say*?'

'I said if Grinling had wanted them eau de nil, he'd have painted them eau de nil in the first place.'

'So what did *she* say?'

'Nothing. She couldn't.'

'Why? I believe she can be quite frosty when she wants.'

'Why? Because I'd already asked her to lunch on Sunday.'

'Brilliant.'

'Yes, it was, wasn't it?'

'Told her who was coming?'

'Certainly.'

'She wouldn't miss it for the world now, surely?'

'No, of course not.'

'But he *won't*. Apparently.'

'Why not?'

Elliott shrugged.

'He *doesn't*. Apparently.'

'Really?'

'No. Hardly ever.'

'Ah well, never mind, I hear he's a bit of a plant bore anyway. So tempis heart.'

They both smiled fleetingly.

Pemberton did not want to go to luncheon with Fulton and

54

Elliott for many reasons. One of them was because he didn't like to sit down to luncheon, on principle, with people whom he was employing in any capacity, and the other was because he didn't like those sort of chaps, and he didn't mind who knew it. They had the same effect on him as cold tapioca. Not that he had any strong prejudices or anything, they just turned his stomach, ever since he'd had to throw a jug at one of them at school. It still brought him out in a sweat to think of it.

Jennifer simply wouldn't leave it at that though, she had to bang on about it.

'Of course I told Elliott you wouldn't be coming,' said Jennifer, 'but only because I did hope that you would.'

This was the sort of statement that Jennifer specialised in, and it was the sort of statement that made Pemberton want to go to his club and read a newspaper, any newspaper.

'Pember, please come to lunch on Sunday, please.'

'No. I've got things to do. Look you go, enjoy yourself. Do you good to talk about bits and pieces. I couldn't, really I couldn't.'

He walked off into the garden, leaving Jennifer to pull a little face behind his back. And then she went to find Nanny and talk about smocking.

Once in the garden Pemberton felt less agitated. Jennifer was some few years younger than he, and it was at times like these the gap of years made itself felt. Also, she had a tendency to middle-class liberalism that he personally deplored. She simply didn't understand that once you let standards slip, all was lost. Of course, it wasn't just the difference in age that was beginning to show itself, the difference in backgrounds was also somewhat more apparent to him now that they had been married a little time. You either were or you weren't, and much as he loved his Jennifer, he feared that she never would quite make it.

Jennifer glanced out of the nursery window at Pemberton. She could just glimpse him from where she stood, and a fine sight he made, with his elegant clothes, his immaculate figure, his tall bearing and his measured tread, as he walked past his favourite piece of garden, but even so, she had to admit, he was dreadfully stuffy. Perhaps he would change. People did. She would have to help in this of course. It was probably all to do with his being an only child, and his mother being so horrible to him; something like that. Whatever the reasons, and they were obviously all boring and psychological, not even an optimist such as herself could possibly expect him to change before Sunday, and she would have to reconcile herself to that, and no two ways about it. She didn't like going out on her own, but not to go would be to give in to Pember, and that would never do.

And so to lunch in her little black BMW, which she loved to distraction. It had special wheels, and her own number plate, and she hadn't loved anything so much since her first doll's pram.

As she drove to Bath, she rehearsed in her mind how she would be to Lady Mary and Lucius, for none of them had even glimpsed each other since Jennifer's wedding to Pemberton, which meant that she would have to be different, because she was very different from the Jennifer Parker-Jones that they had known in former times. She would not be assertive, of course, that would be vulgar. Neither would she be too modest, for Lady Mary, older though she was than Jennifer, did not now have to be treated as someone so terribly special, she was not after all a Marchioness.

As she was too early, she drove round and round Bath until she would be only, correctly, five minutes late, and then she arrived still, she hoped, before the London guests, but not early enough to be disconcerting. She wouldn't have been able to say why, but as soon as she saw the Porsche in front of the front door, she knew she was going to be wrong-footed, and yet she didn't know why she knew it. Something of her old feelings of claustrophobia returned to her, and she thought she might go to a telephone box and ring up on her own behalf, and say that she was unwell, too unwell to attend, which was, in a way, true.

She mounted the stairs to Fulton and Elliott's elegant apartment overlooking one of the finest squares in the city, feeling, as she always used to, that somehow she was being 'set up'. That Fulton and Elliott had only asked her to make fun of her. She had to remind herself that she was as curious to come as they were anxious to ask her.

She breathed in slowly once or twice, and then she walked in the already open door. Necessarily the first person she saw was

Elliott, for he was pouring the champagne into chilled glasses, and so she stood beside him half-hoping that he would tell her that there were no other guests coming, that they had all cried off when they heard she was coming, and it would really be better if she went home now. Unfortunately Elliott said none of these things, but took her firmly into the drawing room where stood Lady Mary and Lucius, both with those yellowy tans that still give people a rich chic, even though sunbathing was not fashionable, as it used to be.

Her carefully rehearsed modest demeanour was quickly forgotten the moment Lady Mary greeted her, for far from having aged, as Jennifer had half-hoped, and as her silly mother had told her, Lady Mary was, if anything, more beautiful. She seemed even taller, as people do when they're looking well, and her funny eye that was strangely speckled and slightly hypnotising was no longer concealed beneath a constant sway of dark hair, but used to create a becoming aura of shyness, a timidity, which was in fact non-existent. Worse than all this, she and Lucius chose to ignore that Jennifer had had any change in fortunes since they had last seen her, and greeted her in that sweetly patronising way, both polite and only half-interested, that was carefully designed to make the recipient want to stamp her foot. She could see that she was still only fat little Jennifer to them and there was no way that she could stop it.

They sat down to luncheon precisely forty minutes after they had arrived. Pemberton had been right in predicting that he would not be needed for there would be plenty of men to go round. Lucius and Lady Mary had brought with them a friend, Hugo, and so everyone had a friend, or friends, except Jennifer. It had been the same at school. Playtime spent alone, or swinging endlessly on deserted swings, or playing horses and ponies on your own. And so it seemed that luncheon was to be spent in much the same way, for she had no one whose little glances made someone else's remark a private joke, no one who murmured a little intimate piece of emotional shorthand, no one who looked across the table through the highly scented flowers at her, and saw the person whom she felt herself to be, wanted herself to be.

Of course they pretended to try and include her in, but with little real success, for dearly as she would have liked to, she did not understand their conversation. She did not know their Bobos and Siggys and Pussys and Beas, all of them strolling elegantly across the heavy white linen tablecloth to be masticated conversationally, their faults laughed at, their tragedies glossed over, their venialities revered, and all of them to flash past Jennifer as so many strangers sitting in an express train.

She found herself dabbing her mouth too frequently with her napkin, and then she found to her consternation that she had dabbed her mouth so frequently that she must now be sitting with that too firm line of red on the outer lips that gives a person the look of someone who has suddenly lost their looks, and become a little mad.

At one point Lady Mary said, 'I don't know if I know any of her friends, do I?'

'Why of course you do,' said Hugo, 'they're the people for whom she never has a good word to say.'

'Yes, yes, of course.'

Jennifer smiled uncertainly as they laughed.

Finally she ran from the lunch just as liqueurs were being offered. She had unfortunately to go back to Charles, her little boy, she said, and everyone pursed their lips sympathetically. She felt he might have a little cold coming on, and she wanted to see if he had a temperature.

They quite understood, as people always do when they are thankfully getting rid of you and Jennifer, clutching her coat over her arm, for she was still a sort of puce magenta in colour, found herself at last down the stairs and on the pavement staring at the outside world as if it was something which for the previous few hours she had feared had been taken away from her. Thankfully the trees were still the same, the sky was still a little the same, and there were ordinary people passing her, no doubt full of roast beef, and Yorkshire puddings, and apple pie, and all those dishes that Pember always insisted on; and they were all just like her and Pember, ordinary people who liked ordinary things. She climbed into her car, carefully shutting her silk dress in the door. Someone had bent her radio aerial into a shape, but it really didn't matter. All that mattered was getting home. She drove off, still buckling her seat belt, as someone does who is being chased.

Fulton watched her from his kitchen window, and then he picked up the coffee tray and went through to the drawing room. Lucius was standing by the looking glass his fourth finger posed lightly upon his thumb. He surveyed the rest of the room with mock gravity.

'Well?'

'*Well*.'

'*Well*.'

It was their little catch phrase at the moment.

Elliott started to laugh.

'I thought if anyone said "eau de nil" once more, I would burst,' he said.

'Don't.'

'I honestly don't think she noticed,' said Mary. 'I don't think she's the kind of person who does.'

'Maybe not,' said Lucius, 'she never used to be the kind of person who noticed.'

'I must say when you said "I love this salad, it's a sort of 'eau de nil', isn't it?" I thought I'd die,' said Fulton, 'I must say I did.'

They all laughed, and laughed. It was after all very funny, which was why they said so several times.

Jennifer could not hear them laughing, but she could imagine them, and she knew she was right in doing so, just as she knew that it was the Tisburys' new Range Rover parked in front of the house when she pulled up at the Hall some forty minutes later.

Pemberton looked determinedly unembarrassed when she came into the drawing room, as he and the Tisburys were still at coffee. He had not told Jennifer that he had asked the Tisburys to drinks in her absence. He did not have to tell her everything, and therefore he had not.

'The Tisburys just popped over for drinks, as I was on my own,' said Pemberton, 'so I thought, since they were here, they might as well stay for some lunch, for lunch.'

He hummed a little tune after he had said this.

'Of course, sweetie,' said Jennifer, 'what a lovely idea. Now you must excuse me, it's Charles. I think he might have a cold.'

'Look a bit flushed yourself, sweetie. Are you all right?'

'Perfectly, thank you,' said Jennifer. 'How are you, Patti?'

'Fine, just fine,' said Patti.

Jennifer went out. Pemberton gave a little sigh. He didn't know why but he had the feeling that he'd done something wrong. Still, best not to think about that now. He looked down at Patti's red plunge dress. She had been a positive feast all through luncheon.

'Let's all go round the garden,' he announced.

But Gerard declined. Quite obviously he had other plans, lucky devil.

Of course Charles had not got a cold, any more than Jennifer had a cold, any more than Nanny had a cold, but nevertheless it was a great relief to climb the nursery stairs and sink into the low wicker chair, and watch him, and talk to Nanny, and discuss things that really mattered such as whether or not he should be allowed boudoir fingers after refusing his brown bread cheese sandwiches? Or whether they should ask any other 'smalls' over to tea next Sunday, or just his little girlfriend in the village?

Normally she threw herself into these nursery discussions because she felt she should, but not today. Today she had learnt a lesson, and that was that she was not the sort of person that she wanted to be, and she never would be. She was plain, and plump, just as her mother had often told her, and she was not able to cope very well outside the limits of her own little life. She knew she might as well be living in one of the cottages on the estate for all she had the ability to become someone such as Lady Mary was. Sophisticated, well-bred, beautiful, someone who would, in all honesty, suit the Hall better, far better than she did. Worse than this realisation was that Pember had warned her just how it would be, in his own funny way. He had banged on, she realised now, not because he just didn't want her to socialise but because he knew, in his kindness, that she could not cope.

She remembered once, when they were very first married, how Pember had tried to make her understand this.

'It's not that I dislike human beings, it's just that I prefer horses. It's not that I don't like being in other people's houses, it's just that I'd rather be in one of my own. And, anyway, what do we do when we socialise? Nothing except tear apart reputations, mock and mimic others, and sell our best friend's secrets for fifty pence worth of gin, and a pound or two's of claret. And if we don't? If only pleasantries are exchanged, and nice things said, we all return home declaring it to have been a dull evening, and not one amusing remark made. Well, damn it, I think that's a very poor way of going on. And if anyone asks me I shall tell them, and so should you.'

Pember was right. It was a very poor way of going on, and yet now, because of her, in her absence, he had turned to asking people up to the Hall. It seemed that she had, by her stupidity, made him change his mind about socialising, just as she had reached the point when she had come to agree with him. She felt so perfectly wretched, only Charles soaking her silly silk frock by his splashings in the bath really cheered her up. Children were so much more interesting than adults. They didn't mock you, or hurt your feelings on purpose. She must have more of them. So many in fact that she would be far too busy wiping noses and bandaging cut knees to be even tempted to leave the house or the estate ever again. Best of all, if she became the mother of a large brood it would annoy her mother, and that surely was incentive enough?

The new Mrs Gillott, in happy ignorance of the Seventh Marchioness of Pemberton's breeding plans for the future, was herself making positive decisions as to acquiring a country house. One of these decisions was based on 'the fact that Andrew, her husband, was badly in need of good fresh air and an isolated spot, where he would be far away from the hideous temptations of the Claremont Club, and other fashionable haunts.

'Don't forget we must go together to choose a country house, poppet,' she was in the habit of reminding him every morning, as he disappeared out of the house.

Andrew, who loathed being called 'poppet' probably as much as he loathed his new wife (not more, that was not possible), paused by the dining room door every morning as she repeated this statement, and made a sort of sound in between a 'yes' and a 'no', and then, tucking his *Daily Telegraph* under his arm, disappeared at a fast trot. He did not want to look at country houses, because it meant being in close proximity with the Mu-Mu Maiden in a motor car for hours on end, and that was not something he could contemplate. His plan was to let her choose the wretched residence, leave her to go to hell there, and beetle back to town.

Unfortunately this was not to be, it seemed, for on the morning of the fifth of that month she called him at the horrendous hour of seven and, after breakfast, just as he was doing his usual escape act with his *Daily Telegraph*, delayed his exit with that particular sharp tone that, in the few short weeks he had had the misfortune to be her spouse, he had come to realise meant business. There was no pussyfooting round this one, for she announced, in that unattractive voice of hers, that not only were they booked to see several houses in Wiltshire but, worst of all horrors, she had a picnic packed and ready and would expect him in the hall, also packed and ready, within the next half an hour.

Memory of the Countess's comforting prediction that a country house would be the answer to all his problems great and small gave Andrew the necessary courage to face being cooped up with his worst beloved in a motor car. It wasn't just that he couldn't stand her. She made such stupid remarks. She talked about the countryside looking very pretty, even if it wasn't. She criticised everyone else's driving, even though she was not capable of driving a car through gateposts five miles wide and, worst of all, she gave him little hints on how to improve his own driving, while making up her face in what she coyly referred to as her 'vanity mirror'.

She was also a route maniac. Her route was always the correct one, even if it wasn't. Her route was the one you always should have taken. Her route was the one with less traffic, no hold-ups, and led you by the best places to stop and have lunch; to crown everything, it even, on one occasion, had better weather. Thinking of all this and steeling himself to face the inevitable, Andrew took the precaution of packing his Georgian hip flask in his back pocket. A little nip of vodka between times would keep him from chucking himself out of the car window.

'Poppet?'

'Yes?'

'Poppet, do you think you should drink from your hip flask while you're driving?'

'I'm not drinking from my hip flask while I'm driving.'

'Don't be babyish, poppet, I just saw you.'

'I am drinking from my hip flask while I'm at the traffic lights, not while I am driving.'

'Yes, but poppet, don't you think it's a bit early? I mean it's only quarter past ten.'

'Not if you've been up since seven it ain't,' said Andrew with feeling. 'If you've been up since seven when you normally don't rise until nine, it is now quarter past twelve, which is a perfectly proper time to have a drink.'

Clarissa sighed and went back to looking out of the window. There was no talking to men, because they simply didn't listen. It would all be very different once they were settled deep in the heart of Wiltshire, only to return to the flat for special occasions such as her birthday, and various 'At Homes' that she would give; but until that halcyon time she had to be patient, and understand that, without any doubt, Andrew was not yet quite as civilised as an ordinary person might wish. He had, after all, been a bachelor for all of his already many years, so marriage could not hope to change him overnight – although it must change him in time, she thought with determination, as she watched him take yet another swig from his hip flask.

The first house that they were to see was an Edwardian reproduction of a Victorian copy of a Gothic cottage. It was hampered by a few drawbacks. The first of these was the house itself, the second was the garden, and the third was its close proximity to a settlement of bungalows which were sited opposite.

'I ain't going in that,' said Andrew.

'Don't be silly, poppet, we've come all this way.'

'No. Rather live in your house in Surrey,' said Andrew tactlessly.

Clarisa sighed.

'Oh very well, I'll go,' she said. 'Someone's got to.'

Andrew climbed back into the car, and took out his now depleted hip flask.

'Bloody woman,' he said to the dashboard.

In the end the bloody woman took so long going round the house he emptied his hip flask and had to stop off at the nearest hostelry to have both himself and it filled up. It was impossible to be cooped up with the Mu-Mu Maiden when travelling without getting completely pissed, thought Andrew, as he steadied himself in the Gents, standing beside a farmer who had not the same degree of control. He sighed. He knew he still had two more houses to go round before he was going to be allowed back into a pub again. It was such a horrendous thought he took another swig from his now replenished hip flask.

'Here we are, poppet,' said Clarissa brightly.

Poppet, looking morose, turned and looked at the house. Unfortunately it was not so bad that he could refuse to go round it.

'Basins and tiled splashbacks in all the rooms, that is good,' said Clarissa, reading from the details before getting out of the car.

Andrew followed her up the drive at a steady pace. He thought the house looked almost passable, but he wouldn't know a tiled splashback if it came up and tapped him on the shoulder, any more than he would a dado if he came across it on an archaeological dig. Clarissa had this way of wafting words around that he had never heard of before, words that he had not been brought up to understand, words that his mother had not used. It wasn't just vanity mirrors, or tiled splashbacks. There were other items, things he'd never seen before, dreadful things such as bidets, and bathmats, and tea cosies, and tray cloths, all details of a life about which he had in former days been happily ignorant. It made him long for the quiet simplicity of life at the Claremont. There a chap dined, a chap played cards, a chap won or lost, but a chap never got what he could only describe as 'embroiled'. Life with Clarissa was most definitely embroiling, he thought, as he fell over the vendor and into her hat stand.

'Oh dear,' said Clarissa out aloud, picking up the vendor, 'I'm awfully afraid my husband isn't himself.'

Alas, she thought, this was so far from the truth to be almost amusing. She left Poppet to pick himself up. It was the least he could do, in the circumstances, considering.

Chapter Five

If Georgiana had a fetish, it was for pretence. Ever since she was a child she had liked to pretend, at odd moments and quite suddenly, that she was someone else. Trotting beside Nanny on long, dull walks which quite obviously bored Nanny as much as they bored her, she would be another child, a child with a much-longed-for dog, or an old magician who could turn Nanny into stone, or a person who could fly away. These escapes from her drab existence would, if successful, enable her to return home to nursery tea in a greatly excited state. Sometimes a fevered flush would appear on her face caused by the intensity of her feelings which, combined with the unusual buoyancy in her manner, would persuade Nanny to take her temperature.

She had greatly disliked Nanny when she was a child, and it was only as an adult that she had grown fond of her, or felt she should be fond of her, because now Nanny was old it would be unfair to dislike her when she was defenceless. Since she had become an adult she had had little reason to pretend to be anyone other than herself (and she was aware that there were people who would willingly become Lady Georgiana Longborough in her place) and so her childish love of pretence lay unawakened until the moment when she started to have an affair with Gus, and invented Lord Longborough.

Lord Longborough was as ogrish as Nanny had been. He did not force her to eat horrendous meals of appalling ingredients, but he did force her to attend them on his behalf. He was flattening as Nanny had been, in that although he did not tell her to stop 'showing off' the moment she smiled, nevertheless, he criticised her publicly. He was mean. (This explained why her flat was not a more elaborate place.) And he was obsessed by the fact that she had not given him an heir in the same way that Nanny had been obsessed by the fact that Georgiana's mother had not given her a boy to bring up.

Happily for Georgiana, deceiving Gus with Lord Longborough was perfectly easy, for neither knew the same people, and Gus cared nothing about the kind of person that Georgiana counted among the people in her small, elegant, navy-blue leather, gold-embossed, initialled address book. If Gus had not made love to her so successfully she knew that she would have been just another instantly forgettable 'Society poodle', as he liked to call girls such as herself.

Once created, the brooding presence of Lord Longborough became as necessary to Georgiana as Gus himself, and as much part of their affair as they themselves. He was the reason she left early in the afternoons, and arrived late in the mornings. For him she had to return to Longborough House at the weekends to play hostess.

'Why don't you tell him to go to hell?' Gus would ask her sometimes, and Georgiana would smile her mischievous smile as if highly entertained by such an outrageous idea, and then regretfully decline the dare. Lord Longborough was rich, and there were no lengths to which he would not go to destroy her if she aroused his suspicions, her manner suggested.

'Oh come on,' Gus would say, absentmindedly stubbing out his cigarette in a small, gold, coffee cup full of turpentine. 'He can't kill you.'

Georgiana, at this point – for the conversation over the months took on a ritualism that was a peculiar comfort to both of them – would smile again, but not her mischievous smile.

'You don't know what they're like,' she once said to Gus.

Gus, who came from what he fondly imagined was a tough background, but which in reality had been luxuriant with doting grandparents who took him to the corner shop for sweeties every Saturday, quite naturally did not know what they were like, and when Georgiana tried to describe the lengths to which she knew certain gentlemen would go to seek revenge, she had no need to pretend, for she had indeed been told what 'they' would be like. Elder sisters of friends left in dreadful circumstances, children plucked from the arms of doting mothers, mothers locked up in discreet asylums having been equally discreetly certified as insane; she had heard enough to know that it wasn't difficult to take on the Establishment in the shape of the law and your husband, it was impossible.

'The working class can be quite bad too, you know doll,' said Gus, for he liked to exaggerate his accent to amuse her.

'It's different.'

'Not when you're holding up a by-pass it's not.'

Georgiana couldn't explain, but looking back she knew that that had been one of the reasons that Kaminski had held such an attraction for her. By the power of his reputation, and for the short duration of their affair, he had built a wall around her, and no one had been able to climb in.

Now of course she might love Gus. She certainly told him so, as people do when they make love, but she did not question what the nature of that love could be, or if it was to be anything more than a fantasy behind a red curtain.

It did not take long for him to start painting her. It was what she had hoped. She brought her velvet cover from her flat and lay across it on the studio bed, in her thick gold collar. The painting he called 'Odalisque', in homage he said, but Georgiana never asked to whom and he did not bother to tell her, knowing it would mean nothing to her.

Her skin was lint white, for she did not believe in sunbathing, and her dark hair touched her shoulders in such a way that she could feel it when she had no clothes on, and it half-mesmerised her, so that she did not at all mind posing for hours on end in comfortable narcissism.

She had never watched a painter before, and she was surprised by how they used their paint, pushing it, working it, making it squeak on the palette. She loved the sounds of the studio and the smell of the turpentine mingling with Gus's cigarettes – even though she loathed nicotine normally, and would leave a table if someone near her smoked, as always when passion is at play, Gus's cigarettes did not offend but were, she told herself, part of his being different. And just as she had never attempted to understand her former lover Kaminski, so now she did not attempt to understand this sculptor, this painter, this man apart from her world, with whom she was having an affair. Perhaps it was part of Georgiana's appeal that she did not have any desire to entangle herself in the mentality of a man, butaccepted that he was different, that he had desires which weren't hers, thoughts that weren't hers, and although she was not indifferent to what these might be, at the same time she was incurious.

'You don't have to go.'

Every Friday afternoon he stood in front of the door to stop her going, daring her to return to that boring, stuffy, husband of hers. How could she spend the weekend with him when she spent the week with Gus?

'Telephone the old bastard, for Christ's sake.'

Gus blasphemed constantly, and without thought. In fact he used bad language in such a commonplace way that Georgiana had come to think of it, as she thought of his smoking and his disregard for possessions, as something that proved that he was real, that he was proper. Nevertheless she sensed that should she ever give in to him and stay for the weekend, telephone the 'old bastard' and make her excuses, Gus would in all probability find having her around terribly tiresome; instead of which, leaving him as she did made her seem exciting. By Monday he longed for her. Besides, he enjoyed getting himself into a state. Sometimes he would take it too far.

'We can't have this every week.'

'We can't have this every week,' he mimicked her voice. 'And why can't we have this every week? Because it's not the way to go on, is it, Lady Longborough? Why are you so useless at expressing yourself?'

He threw a paint rag at the canvas.

Georgiana looked at him.

'I think, actually, *it* is useless.'

He swore. She went. And then he returned to his easel.

'Odalisque' was coming on. He turned the canvas nearer the light. He was gradually simplifying the slim rounded body, capturing her grave expression, full of formality, as if at an Ascot picnic, not lying around on a fur rug without her clothes.

'Little whore, aren't you?' he asked the painting.
And moments later he left the studio to get drunk.

Chapter Six

'She's got no stick, that's the trouble,' muttered Sir Gerard, as he watched Patti sliding slowly off her horse's back and on to the grass.

'I think I've hurt myself,' gasped Patti.

'You either have or you haven't,' said Sir Gerard.

'I have, I've hurt myself.'

Patti looked round slowly at her husband in the forlorn hope that he might come across and help her up. But this was not to be expected from Sir Gerard, who merely stood watching her and then walked across to the horse, who was on the end of a lunge rein, and patted his neck.

'You all right, old fellow?' he asked.

Patti sighed. She was going into the house, and she was going to have a drink, and then she was going to tell Knightey just what she thought of the horse he'd bought her.

Sir Gerard watched her walking slowly back to the house. He ought to make her climb back on board again, but he couldn't face it. She'd been out the back door four times that morning. Four times! It didn't seem possible for someone to fall off a horse so many times in exactly the same way, and at a slow trot. Her toes turned down, her bottom turned up, and her head poked forward so that she looked like a pecking hen. She was all wrong; on the ground all right, on a horse all wrong. Not like his first wife, who looked so elegant on her horse that it would stir a chap's heart to see her, it was when she got off the animal that she made you a bit thoughtful.

He walked up the field holding the horse.

'Couple of old fools with a young fool,' he said to the horse.

He was a nice old chap, as safe as houses, what is always described as a 'schoolmaster'. You could let off a firecracker beside him and he'd stand like a rock, pick up his feet, do anything with him in the stable, he just couldn't keep the wife on him, but that wasn't his fault. Somewhere, above them, a cuckoo called. By and by there would be summer, and perhaps with summer Patti's 'stick' would improve.

Patti lowered herself into the bath. She had enjoyed buying her riding clothes, she had enjoyed being bought a horse, but she did not enjoy having to ride. It was too painful. And hating heights as she did, it gave her vertigo to look down and see the ground seemingly so far away. Knightey always got so cross whenever she climbed up on Havoc. Shout, shout, shout, that's all he could think of doing. She was quite sure that making a person walk about on top of a horse without a saddle did not improve your riding. She was quite sure that it was just one of Knightey's silly, old-fashioned ideas, but how could she tell him? She would if she knew something about horses, but since she didn't, she couldn't. She had bought a book from Smiths entitled *How To Ride Easily*, so as to try and learn from the pictures, but big G. had just laughed at it, which was silly and cruel of him, because at least the book didn't shout at you and didn't make you fall off.

Downstairs someone rang the bell. It intoned solemnly, echoing round the cellar where it was housed in old-fashioned isolation.

Patti wrapped herself in her dressing gown. She knew it was Mrs Dupont. There were some people who had to call and there were some people who never called, Mrs Dupont was the first. She was always just 'dropping by'.

'Oh dear, did I catch you?'

'No really, it's all right,' said Patti.

Mrs Dupont gave a small laugh of a harsh nature when she saw Patti was still in her dressing gown.

'Still in bed, are we?'

'Wish I was.'

'Oh Lady Tisbury, you are funny.'

'Not really,' said Patti, 'I just fell off that wretched Havoc,

71

and this bum of mine don't half hurt.'

Mrs Dupont now doubled herself up laughing.

'Oh don't, Lady Tisbury. You're too funny for words. No, listen, I just called to say thank you *so* much for the invitation, and Geoffrey and I would *love* to come to your soirée on the twentieth.'

'You would? Great. See you then.'

Patti shut the front door quickly, and ran back up to her bathroom. She climbed back into the hot water, and lay her head on the pink plastic bath cushion that she had had since she was fifteen. Her guest list for what Mrs Dupont had just called her 'soirée' was now almost complete. Everyone was coming, which was another peculiarity of the country. In London you asked everyone, and no one came, or anyway only half of the invited, but in Wiltshire you asked everyone, and they only went and turned up.

At lunch Gerard said, 'They're nosey, that's all. Don't think they're coming for any other reason, do you?'

'I don't know,' said Patti truthfully.

'Course not,' said Gerard. 'They want to see what you're like, what I'm like, what the house is like, and then they want to go away and talk about it, and hope they won't have to ask you back.'

Patti looked round the now completed dining room with its heavy quilted tenting, and its ornate patterns.

'But Knightey, I don't want them to talk about it, I want them to like it.'

'Don't be a fool, pet, no one ever wants to like another chap's house, much better if they don't. Know the story about the King of France?'

Patti shook her head. He always liked to ask her if she knew things when he knew she didn't.

'King of France had a Minister who built himself a glorious house. Did it up from top to toe, the lot, and when it was finished what could be more natural than to ask his King to dinner, which he duly did. Follow me?'

Patti nodded.

'And the King came to dinner, and when he saw how magnificent this chap's house was, he went away and gave orders to cut the fellow's head off.'

72

'Why? Didn't he like the house?'

'On the contrary, my sweet, he loved the house, that was it, you see, it was better than his own, so just think about that next Saturday, and you won't feel so bad.'

Sir Gerard lit a cigar and then, rising from the dining room table, he walked away leaving his chair out and his napkin on the floor. Patti remained seated. She frowned and stared at the fruit bowl. She didn't know why but she had no idea at all what the King of France had to do with her housewarming party? Sometimes Knightey went a bit too fast for her, and just now was one of those times.

'She's only bought a house,' said Jennifer dramatically, flinging down a letter.

'Who's bought a house?' asked Pemberton.

'Mrs Gillott,' said Jennifer through tightened lips, because since her mother's remarriage she used this form of address for her. 'Mrs Gillott has only bought a house just thirty miles away, which means she can come and call ad nauseam.'

'Thirty miles is quite far. Not too near.'

'Not far enough, and far too near,' said Jennifer.

Pemberton, who had quite approved of his mother-in-law remarrying on the grounds that it would keep his old friend Gillott out of mischief, didn't have a reply ready at this point. He knew Jennifer's mother acted on her nerves like a nail on a blackboard and now that Jennifer was pregnant again the situation could not hope to improve. He smiled across the breakfast table at her. She was a wonderful little woman. He only had to look at her to get her pregnant, a marvellous facility in that direction. Of course he'd like a second son to make the title quite secure, and he was sure that she would oblige.

'Yours sincerely and oblige,' he said out aloud.

'What did you say, Pember?'

Jennifer threw her mother's letter on to the dining room fire.

'I said "Yours sincerely and oblige",' said Pemberton.

'But why? Why did you say "Yours sincerely and oblige," Pember?'

'I don't know,' said Pemberton truthfully. 'I think it was

because I couldn't think of anything else to say.'

'In that case I think it was rather a silly thing to say, Pember.'

'Do you? You're probably right, but I've always wondered what it meant? You know, tradesmen put it on the end of letters.'

'I am perfectly well aware that tradesmen put it on the end of letters,' said Jennifer. 'What I'm not aware of is why you should sit there saying something that tradesmen put on the end of letters.'

'Never mind,' said Pemberton, 'let's just get on with the day, shall we?'

Jennifer got up and pushed her chair into the table. He watched her. She was a bit snappy and what grooms call 'mareish', and so on, at the moment, only to be expected in her condition. He could forgive that. What he couldn't forgive was the fact that even when she wasn't pregnant she was inclined to be stuffy about funny things. She couldn't just be plain silly, or even a bit silly. She always had to be told why something silly was funny, and even then she wouldn't find it funny, she'd find it silly. And then she couldn't play around with words, or see why something out of place at the wrong time was funny rather than irritating. It was the tradesman in her. Although of course he couldn't say so, but it was obvious. Tradesmen were always so busy adding things up and counting the cost of everything that was worthless, they could never see when anything was priceless.

The new baby would arrive just in the nick of time, he felt, for of late his mood had been somewhat autumnal in contrast to the deepening spring outside. There was no real reason for this of course, just a feeling which, together with a vague unrest, was making him awaken earlier than was normal for him and go to sleep later than usual. It was as if something was about to happen, something he hadn't planned.

'Apparently it is bow tie for the Tisburys' soirée tonight,' said Jennifer at the end of the following week. 'Can you imagine what it's going to be like?'

Pemberton did not bother to reply for he had been subjected to a relentless campaign against the Tisburys ever since he had had the temerity to ask them to stay for Sunday lunch.

74

'I'm sure she's never given a black-tie affair before,' she went on. 'I mean, she doesn't look as if she'd know how to organise it, does she?'

'I'm just going to see Bloss about something,' said Pemberton, and he escaped through the drawing room door leaving Jennifer to contemplate the fact that her mother and step-father were arriving after lunch to spend the weekend, and would also have to be taken to the Tisburys, which was a dreadful thought, for if Mrs Gillott decided to wear her lime green patterned there would be no doubt about it but that the Seventh Marchioness of Pemberton would be the laughing stock of her own village, and she would probably have to go and live in their Norfolk house for the rest of the pregnancy, which would not be amusing. The very idea of it made her have to go upstairs and have a lie-down.

'I have no idea why Jennifer thought it necessary to change the hall,' said Clarissa later, turning round and looking to Pemberton for sympathy.

Pemberton, who had had no idea, either at the time or subsequently, wanted to agree but he was unable to, for loyalty to Jennifer forbade his being able to agree with Jennifer's mother on any subject whatsoever, even the weather . . .

'I think it looks charming,' he said with an effort.

'It looked so nice before,' said Clarissa, 'and now, now it looks like a nightclub.'

'How about a drink, drinks everyone?' asked Pemberton.

'Thought you'd never ask,' said Andrew heavily.

He followed Pemberton into the library, leaving Clarissa to follow if she would, which he devoutly hoped she wouldn't, and which happily she did not.

'How's it going, old chap?' asked Pemberton as they both walked the well-worn path to the old oak table that held the drinks.

'What? What going?' asked Andrew completely at sea, because he could only think of a large gin and not too much tonic at that precise moment.

'Your marriage, you know, how's IT going?'

'It? It's frightful.'

'At least you're getting it.'

'That's the frightful part.'

'How ghastly.'

'It is, it's ghastly.'

'Frightful.'

'No, it's not, it's worse, it's ghastly.'

'Yes, and frightful for you.'

'Oh yes it's frightful for me all right, that's what's so ghastly about it.'

'Ghastly. Have another gin.'

'I think I'll have to.'

'Yes, I will too.'

They both murmured 'throw the first one down, and sip the second' as was their custom when they were alone, which alas tonight they were not going to be for very long.

It was a strange business being married, Pemberton reflected, because it so often came between you and everything else, and yet on paper there was no real reason why it should. After all, in his particular case, marriage had had no reason to change him, except in that he now had a woman in the house, his house, but all other vital statistics had stayed exactly as they were, the staff, his interests, himself, all these other things should have stayed exactly as they were since they were, on the surface of things, unchanged. But such was not the case, he had to admit, such was not the case at all. He did not add 'alas', because he had no need to.

'Women, it's women that change marriage, marriage would be all right without women,' said Andrew, 'they've always got to be doing something or saying something, and that changes everything. You can't even read a book without them interrupting you. It's hell, I tell you, absolute hell.'

'While I'm very happy myself,' said Pemberton with caution, 'nevertheless, I do see your point of view, particularly in the light of what you just told me. It must be ghastly.'

'Ghastly,' said Andrew, 'but' he added, 'it'll be all right, once I've got rid of her.'

'Yes,' agreed Pemberton, 'that'll make things much better for you.'

'Time to change,' called Clarissa through the door.

Andrew remained seated.

'Andrew!'

Clarissa's voice now became harsh, of a harshness which was quite indescribable, unless you'd actually heard it for yourself. Pemberton looked at Andrew hoisting himself to his feet. Poor old chap, he might be a complete idiot, but he quite obviously didn't deserve Jennifer's mother.

'See you later, old chap,' said Andrew.

Pemberton watched him dragging himself out of the room, and a deep and frightening sadness settled right in the middle of him, as if life was no longer worth living, as if it was a match that could never be won, as if you always paid for everything you enjoyed. That was how bad watching Andrew leave the room made him feel. Only minutes later Jennifer put her head around the door and, in a suddenly all too familiar way, summoned Pemberton also to dress.

'Not another drink Pember, surely?' asked Jennifer, who had become very conscious of people's drinking habits since she had become pregnant again.

'Yes, another drink,' said Pemberton boldly, and he poured himself very deliberately a large double.

'I don't think you should, you know, Pember.'

'You don't think I should *what*?' asked Pember, making it even a little more than a double.

'I don't think you should have another before you go up. It's frightfully ageing, you know. Drinking constantly is very ageing.'

If he hadn't been a gentleman Pemberton would have said 'oh balls', but since he was, he didn't, but thought it instead, and then he went 'up'. Tonight he didn't care if he aged, or got drunk for that matter. At least he had one thing to which he could look forward, and that was 'Lady Tizzy', as he now called her. He could look forward to Lady Tizzy and her glorious shape. He went 'up', but slowly, and he took his drink.

On seeing her mother's dress when they all came 'down', Jennifer wondered how she could have had the cheek to criticise the way she, Jennifer, had re-arranged the hall. Being criticised by a person of taste was just something you had to accept, she had after all had to bow to the circumstance of Elliott's greater taste and knowledge in respect of the library, but being

77

criticised by someone of evidently dreadful taste was not just a punishment, it was a martyrdom.

It was not that her mother wore cheap clothes, she wore expensive clothes, clothes that came from shops that everyone could immediately recognise were very expensive, but she wore all the wrong clothes from those shops, and she wore them with all the wrong things from the other shops. Her clothes didn't look as if she was wearing them, they were very definitely wearing her, but it was not as bad as it could have been, at least the lime-green patterned had been left at home. She had spared Jennifer the necessity of going to live at her house in Norfolk.

Clarissa's private manner towards Jennifer was still as master to servant but her public manner, since Jennifer's marriage, had changed. It was not adopted except when a member of the staff was present. As soon as this happened, Clarissa became overwhelmingly respectful, in order to emphasise her daughter's new position to any or everybody present who just might not be aware of it. This coy awareness was the nearest Jennifer came to receiving anything in the way of kindness from her mother, and it had a wonderful nauseous effect upon her.

Andrew did not join the ladies in the drawing room, but pretended that he thought they were all to go to the library; this was so that he could fill his hip flask from Pemberton's drink tray. The Mu-Mu Maiden had tried to find his hip flask before he could, and spoil his fun, but he had anticipated this and had been able to conceal it somewhere he knew even she would not look – in the old metal cistern in their bathroom. It was still slightly damp, so he wiped it vigorously on his silk handkerchief and then, with a hand so steady it would have done a teetotaller credit, he filled the silver and glass bottle with vodka and a pinch of french, and slipped the elegant little flask into his back pocket. All was thankfully accomplished before Jennifer came into the library to check that the fire had not gone out.

'We're not in here you know, Andrew,' she said as she proceeded to ruin what had been a very healthy fire.

'Sorry?'

'I said, "We're not in here",' said Jennifer again.

'No?' asked Andrew, looking up from an old copy of *Horse*

and Hound that couldn't possibly hold any interest for him.

'No,' said Jennifer, 'we're not in here, we're in the drawing room.'

'Very well,' said Andrew, but he did not move.

'Are you happy, Andrew?' she asked him suddenly.

Andrew, who did not dislike Jennifer as much as he disliked her mother, but rather pitied her because she was not a pretty girl although she seemed to suit Pemberton all right, was surprised that she should even be interested in his state of being.

'How do you mean? Happy, how do you mean?'

Andrew cleared his throat. He couldn't stand the Mu-Mu Maiden and he was utterly miserable, but he knew his duty, and to admit to either state would be a crime, a crime against all the codes that he recognised. Besides, if he let on to the Mu-Mu Maiden's daughter that he disliked her mother, it would spoil all his divorce plans. Bang would go his cover. He must not admit to 'irreconcilable differences' until such time that he was assured that the deeds of the new country house were in that most reassuring of marital states, joint names.

'Of course I'm happy,' he said.

Jennifer stared at him. She knew that he had married her mother to escape certain debts, the whole of London knew that was the reason, and neither she nor London could blame him, but she did blame him for not admitting that he was unhappy. She could not forgive a lack of truth in someone. Truth was all important in Jennifer's life, and she was often shocked that so few people adhered to it. Worse than that, they had a blithe disregard for it, substituting for conversations that they had had ones that they knew that they had never had, and admitting to feelings that only yesterday they had categorically denied. Truth was all important. Andrew was untruthful. He could not be admired.

And so they went through to the drawing room. Jennifer was feeling unwell, and if she didn't think it would put Pember in a huff, she would cry off, but Pember did not understand just how unwell being pregnant could make you feel, but regarded it as a perfectly healthy state to be in, which even if it was so, nevertheless could make you feel distinctly unhealthy. She was not one of his mares, and even if she had been, she would find that any complaints would fall upon ears that could not hear. Pregnancy was a natural process, even if it made you feel very unnatural on occasions. Besides, it being the Tisburys' party – the wretched, wretched Tisburys whom she wished now she had never asked to drinks – because it was them, it made it even more necessary to survive the next few hours without grumbling, for the Tisburys for unknown reasons had turned into Pember's people of the moment.

'Well?'

'*Well*.'

'Everyone's coming, but everyone.'

Fulton paused momentarily to look at Elliott's reflection in the looking glass, and Elliott paused momentarily to look at Fulton's reflection in the same place.

'How's Lady Tizzy? Having hysterics?'

'Not at all. The thing about Lady Tizzy is that she has a great deal of sang froid, and most of it's laid out on the table for buffet, dear.'

Elliott laughed.

'Not cold cuts? I can't bear it.'

'Listen, the only thing chaud that Lady Tizzy's heard of is boiling water, as in "place the bag in boiling water", courtesy of Saint Michael, her patron saint.'

'Will I do?' asked Elliott.

'I'd do you myself if I had the time, but there's the intercom.'

Outside, down below, Lucius looked at Mary. She was quite, quite beautiful. He looked at Hugo. He was quite, quite beautiful. He loved them both utterly. How could he explain to anyone how three people could live in such harmony, share such happiness with each other? No one could understand, and they never would. So much so that he had even made a vow never to write about it, because it would be impossible to do so and get it absolutely right.

'Thank heavens we're all going together,' said Elliott as they went into the drawing room. 'It would be intolerable otherwise.'

'Shall we play the party game?'

'Yes,' said Fulton, 'let's play Spot the Beast.'

'I don't think we know that one,' said Lady Mary.

'Well?'

'*Well*. It goes like this. You choosez for yourself the "beast" at the party, because there is always one "beast" who should never have been asked. And then you keep the name to yourself and afterwards you put it in an envelope, and if your choice gets the most votes you win.'

'What's the prize?' asked Hugo.

'The prize should be the most beautiful person at the party,' said Fulton, and looked him straight in the face, and smiled.

Hugo, who was already the most beautiful person there, also smiled.

'That does sound fun,' said Lady Mary. 'Great fun. Do you know who else is coming, Elliott?'

'The Pembertons, of course, and the dreary old Browns—'

'There's a beast for a start.'

'Don't.'

'I've got an awful feeling they're all going to be beasts, do you know?' said Elliott.

'Good, good, that'll make the competition all the more exciting. It'll be a close run thing.'

'Let's just hope that she has decent drink,' said Hugo.

'Yes, yes, that's all right, I asked. One of the good things about Lady Tizzy is that she is at all times a champagne girl. Poor old Knightey –'

'Who?'

'That's what she calls Sir G.'

'I don't believe it.'

'Yes. Well, she bleeds the poor old fellow dry with her champagne orders. Now. One other thing. I'd rather not anyone said a thing about the decor, not a thing. Because, as Elliott knows, there was not a thing I could do about it. She could not be persuaded, she insisted on everything, and well you know how it is, one gets fed up arguing.'

Everyone knew how it was.

'Come on baby darling,' Patti called up the stairs to Knightey. 'I want to have a drink with you before the guests come.'

Baby darling groaned. He could not do up his bow tie, and

what was worse, Patti could not do up his bow tie, because she was under the impression that all bow ties had hooks at the back. He passed a piece of the wretched thing through the back, and gave it a tug, and then sat down exhausted with the whole effort. He still had to shoe horn his evening shoes, and then there was the beastly business of his having to smile at everyone, and look as if he was enjoying himself.

'Never mind,' he said out aloud to himself, 'it'll all be over by tomorrow.'

He had spent the whole week saying this but inserting the appropriate day of the week instead of 'tomorrow'. He had said it on Monday, Tuesday, Wednesday and Thursday. He had said it in the vegetable garden, in the fields, behind the dung heap, at the back of the horses' boxes, and he had said it with the same rousing conviction that he sang the National Anthem and for the same reason, to encourage himself.

Of course Patti was looking ravishing, but then she always did. She was displaying as much of herself as was permissible in the evening. Perhaps even just a little more. Once she was off a horse he could honestly say that she was a perfectly glorious sight, flowing hair, glowing skin, everything just where it should be. He raised his glass of champagne.

'Here's to fun,' he said.

Patti smiled. Knightey's bow tie was all wobbly, but there wasn't much point in telling him. It would only spoil the moment. He was such a darling, she wouldn't want to spoil anything for him, for it was he who had made everything possible for her, ever since they'd first met at the cocktail lounge.

Her hand went up to her new necklace. Knightey had given it to her especially for this evening. He was a funny old thing, always seeing things in magazines, and sending off for them for her, bless him. It seemed to give him a thrill, the old silly, but nothing would match the thrill of his very first present to her, a little silk cushion with embroidery on it. He was an old angel really, even if he did have a horrid temper and snore.

The guests had started to arrive, barely minutes after they had downed their first glass of champagne, and as they came through the door, stoles wrapped round the ladies, evening scarfs trailing from the men, Gerard realised with a sort of sickening thud that he had left the most important item of all to Patti, and with what horrendous results he would not as yet know – he had left her to invite the guests. She had therefore, quite obviously, asked everyone she had ever talked to since their arrival from London and so, wobbling through the door with apparent amazement, although for different reasons, came the Pembertons together with Mrs Dupont from the village, and the lady who ran the village shop with the Hon. Andrew Gillott. Patti had no social references. She could not know, did not know, whom to ask with whom. Gerard seized his third drink, and it swiftly followed his second.

The party from Bath arrived to be greeted by the invigorating sight of their host aiming peanuts down Mrs Dupont's décolletage.

'Well,' said Fulton.

'*Well*,' said Elliott, and they both turned round and looked at Lady Mary and Hugo.

'It's obviously going to be a hall party,' said Lady Mary to Patti, as she took a glass of champagne from one of the Pembertons' farm workers, who had been hired to 'hand round' for the evening, and was doing so as if he was hurling hay at the cows instead of champagne at humans.

'I beg your pardon?' said Patti.

'A hall party,' said Lady Mary, 'you know how it is, by some unseen rule all the people asked to a party decide at one and the same time where the party is to be held, and there, willy nilly, it is held, be it in the hall, or the kitchen, or the upstairs attic.'

'But I want everyone to see Fulton's lovely decor,' said Patti.

'Don't worry, they'll see everything they want to. People always do.'

'Fulton did it all, you know?' said Patti admiringly.

Fulton raised his eyes to heaven, denying any part of anything, least of all the wallpaper in the hall. Patti saw him, and for a second she was hurt.

'You're not going to be snotty about your own taste, are you Fulton?' she asked, feigning an Upper Class accent.

Fulton retreated.

'Lady Tizzy being naughty,' he said to her.

'Silly thing,' said Patti, 'you know you wouldn't let me choose anything. You know you said I was tasteless.'

But the conversation had to be left there, because Sir Gerard had now aimed and fired a peanut down her own magnificent poitrine.

Lady Mary was already moving on with what she was aware was practised grace. A superb hostess herself, she knew exactly how to perform at other people's parties. How to ease tiny tensions and move away from brewing squalls. How to spot someone who was being boring and send amusing relief to the victim. She was intensely interested in being entertained, and consequently applied herself to each social function that she attended with proper devotion. Tonight was particularly important to her, because she knew that if something sensational happened she could telephone it to the Countess in the morning and that would please her mother. Mary wanted to please her mother and because of this, quite naturally, she never did.

Pemberton, as he arrived, saw at once, or thought he saw at once, what Lady Tizzy had been up to with her guest list, and immediately took it to be an hilarious joke against the County, but since he had never had the opportunity to socialise with anyone from the village, or the woman who ran the cleaners in Stanton, or tall Fred who did windows, he plunged into conversation with them with the genuine enthusiasm of a man who has been deprived of hearing about real life for all too long. Taking their cue from the Seventh Marquis, the rest of the company put their social shoulders to the wheel, and the atmosphere at Flint House turned from unease to hilarity.

After supper Lady Mary, walking through the wild garden, remarked upon the brightness of the moon.

'No one writes about the moon any more, do they?' she asked. 'When I was younger everyone wrote about the moon.'

Hugo put one finger on her smooth, bare arm, and watched its progress to her elbow.

'It's ever since they put that horrid American flag on it. The moon has now become a political statement.'

'Let's pretend it's just the moon,' said Mary.

'Let's pretend you love me,' said Hugo.

Mary's hair covered her face as she bent down and picked a flower from the lawn.

'You know I love you, Hugo.'

'But I want you to love me more than Lucius.'

'That wouldn't be fair. Lucius loves us both.'

'Love is not a school rule.'

'No, but nevertheless it does have its rules.'

'Only that there are no rules. You can invent them as you go along.'

'Not this player can't,' said Mary.

'But you've never played this game before.'

Hugo's finger began its second descent down her arm. It was vaguely pleasurable.

'True. Look, don't let's talk about it any more. Let's talk about the moon again.'

'No, don't let's, let's look for stars that we know. Easy ones like the Great Bear and the Little Bear.'

'How can three people love each other?'

'I don't know, but we do.'

They walked on through the garden brilliantly lit by the political statement from above.

'Three as one,' said Hugo dreamily.

Andrew Gillott sitting on a bench in the rose garden could hear every word.

'They've both gone starkers,' he told his hip flask, and wandered off to have a sleep in the stables.

Sir Gerard, much later, as his mother's small carriage clock struck two o'clock and he shut the gate behind the last of the guests, realised to his astonishment that the party had been an unqualified success, as parties often are when there is unlimited champagne, and the will to drink it. Everyone had enjoyed themselves, that was obvious, and everyone had something to talk about the following day, and would undoubtedly do so. He smiled at the shrubs at the side of the drive and felt happy; then walked slowly and a little unevenly towards the stables. The horses were asleep, but nevertheless he could hear their little nighttime noises. Tomorrow everything would be peaceful again, and he would be able to go for a hack and think of nothing more nor less than the countryside around him, and the horse beneath him.

Patti was waiting to have one last drink and a little chat with him before they went up to bed.

'You know, I'm not sure that we should have played "Spot the Willy", Knightey.'

'Nonsense,' said Sir Gerard. 'They loved it.'

'Yes, yes, they did, didn't they?' agreed Patti. 'You were very good. No one guessed *you*!' she added with pride.

'Well they wouldn't, would they?' said Sir Gerard. 'Stands to reason. I used a Walls banger.'

'Oh Knightey, you're so clever,' sighed Patti.

'No I'm not,' said Sir Gerard, not meaning it.

'Yes you are, you know all about the King of France, and party games, and how to do the crossword in ink.'

'I'm just older than you,' said Sir Gerard. 'Lived longer, that's all. Coming riding tomorrow, or rather this morning?'

'No, I don't think so,' said Patti, 'I think I might have a little headache in the morning.'

'Champagne Charlie, eh?'

'That's it.'

'Not going to have a headache all day, are you?'

'No, of course not!'

Sir Gerard sighed gratefully.

The Countess was being pettish. She was down at her country house, and feeling left out because she had not been asked to the Tisburys' party. Lady Mary tried to smooth her ruffled feelings by telephoning her.

'Do you want to hear about it?' she asked her mother, settling herself back against five white lace pillows and staring at the telephone in her hand as if she was trying to hold the Countess's attention in person.

'Was it beastly and vulgar?' asked the Countess.

'No it was much better than that, it was a sensation,' said Mary.

'How could it be a sensation?' asked the Countess. 'They haven't enough money to give a sensation.'

'The guest list was a riot,' said Mary, and then suddenly

86

realised that this was extraordinarily tactless since it hadn't included the Countess.

'My saxifrage's out,' said the Countess. 'I can just see it from the window.'

'There was John Pemberton and ourselves, and the Pembertons' guests, and then wonderful people like the man who cleans the windows – dear Lady Tizzy, she has no idea.'

'Of course it's always gone on,' said the Countess.

'And then after the buffet everyone played "Spot the Willy".'

The Countess let a tiny pause intervene.

'Spot the Who?'

'No, nothing to do with the Who,' said Mary, '"Spot the Willy". You know, they hold a sheet up and –'

'Oh that,' said the Countess disparagingly, 'everyone used to play that before the war. That's frightfully old hat. And then it became frightfully middle class, and only played by people weekending at Cooden Beach.'

'Sir Gerard won. No one could guess his.'

Mary laughed. Her mother did not laugh in return. Being second to the news of a party was not her idea of how things should be. Mary stopped laughing, since laughing on your own was a false sort of laughter, and made you feel as if the smile was permanent, and the sound repetitive.

'Well, I'd better go,' she said, suddenly sad. 'You know how it is, Fulton doesn't like the telephone being used too much, even though it is Sunday.'

She replaced the receiver.

The Countess replaced hers.

'Of course it's always gone on,' she said with satisfaction to no one at all.

Chapter Seven

The organdie of spring had lifted, and summer's satin was shining through, giving Georgiana a dislike of pavements and motor cars and dull little summer dresses in windows. Once summer came upon the city, the city's grey, the city's dirt and the city's tiresome avarice oppressed. She wanted to be in the fields at Longborough looking with sleepy eyes through blades of grass, and wondering if she had enough energy to pick up a tray and return to the house and fetch another jug of Pimms? And so, with the departures of her parents to Portugal and Nanny to Norfolk, she took Gus down to Longborough.

She had told him that 'Lord Longborough' was away, that he was travelling in Italy, and gambled on the fact that once surrounded by the colours of summer Gus would paint, and when Gus painted she could come and go, and he would be quite unable to say who had come and who had gone, because although she was not artistic she understood that the practice of it was enthralling.

Naturally there were a great many details concerning the evocation of 'Lord Longborough' to be attended to before Gus arrived. She took some of her father's clothes and she hung them in her cupboards (after all, he was meant to be older than she). His monogrammed evening slippers she left out thoughtlessly in her bedroom, his cigarettes in her drawing room, and his Barbour and his riding boots in the cloakroom. She put a white towelling dressing-gown of hers, but which would fit a man, in the bathroom that was 'his', and she imagined that out of tact she would have hidden all photographs of 'Lord Longborough', so that Gus would not be curious.

One detail of which she was proud was the tantalus of after-shave and bath lotions that she bought on 'Lord Longborough's' behalf. It was inconsistent with the gentleman that she had invented and so had a convincing air of truth about it, because she knew that no man is a whole, unless he is completely false. She poured a little from each bottle down the loo, and contemplated with satisfaction this detail of the man to whom she was supposedly married, who was so authoritarian, so demanding, and so selfish, but who had perhaps this servant's taste in scent.

The excitement she felt as she waited for Gus to arrive was as intense as any wife who was actually deceiving her husband. Every minute spent in this man's company would be stolen, a result of careful dishonesty, with the difference that Georgiana had constructed her falsities to conceal a state of innocence. She did not imagine that should he discover the truth Gus would become violent, or that he would stop the affair, but she did think that his passion would become tempered, his fierce possession of her casual, and she would no longer be able to reward him with herself.

'What a beautiful place.'

Gus looked at the house, the gardens, the countryside widening beyond. The farms in the distance, placed in little clusters to enhance the horizon, and confirm the presence of the countryside.

'And how many people's houses did your ancestors have to pull down to build this?' he asked.

Georgiana sighed inaudibly. If he was going to be dull he could go straight back to town, and she could be dull on her own, which was always a luxury in comparison to being dull with someone else.

'It's so warm, I thought we'd have tea on the lawn.'

'Very well, mi'lady.'

'Cucumber sandwiches, and lemon sponge cake. It's all prepared.'

She turned to go in.

'And Indian tea, I hope?'

Indian tea with Gus was not a drink, it was a nationality.

Once or twice when she had persuaded him to try China tea he had drunk it in such a way that suggested that should he be caught doing so, he would be blackballed from the Arts Club. Longborough had done its best to appeal to Gus, it had worn its flowers, its lawns, and its views with all the grace that it could muster, but still he had been unable to look at it without wondering upon what human suffering it had been built? It was as if he had stood at the bottom of a great staircase and watched a beautiful girl coming towards him, and only seen that her mascara was smudged.

Georgiana had not learnt to cook, but she had learned to arrange food. For dinner she had prepared a cuisine that was both fashionable and nouvelle, without being the slightest effort. Little plates of smoked chicken with raddichio arranged decoratively, grilled lamb chops with salad, and some cheese and a sorbet. She moved quietly between the table and the kitchen to heighten the feeling that they were both being waited upon.

Gus did not appreciate the dinner. In fact, although he ate he might as well not have, for he ate without appetite and looked caged and uncomfortable at the end of the table. And although he drank his wine, it did not seem to mellow him.

'Is something the matter?'

'Yes.'

Georgiana looked through the candlelight at him. Gus lit a cigarette.

'I keep feeling that that bastard that you're married to is going to come in,' he said. 'I don't think it's going to work.'

'How do you mean?'

'Being here with you, you know, being here. I don't think it's going to work. I keep wondering if you chose all this, or if he did?'

He looked round the dining room.

'Those buggers – I suppose they're all his sodding ancestors,' he said, 'and this is all his old family silver and well, I don't know. I hate the whole thing. I mean, Christ, you can see what sort of person he is by the way this place is done up. I don't suppose he gave you a chance. I don't suppose the bastard allowed you to have a say. You can see that. You couldn't have chosen all this, only an old bastard like him could have done that.'

Georgiana looked round the dining room which she had spent months getting right, and she knew that they were not inhabiting the same world. In her eyes the dining room was beautiful. The overall colour was warm, a mixture of plum and pink which looked properly faded. The furniture was mahogany, the silver a mixture of Georgian and nearly un-detectable Edwardian, and the glass was pretty and old. Admittedly the ancestors were not of the first water, but then not unnaturally her parents had the best of those. Still, even so, not a room to which one could object. She couldn't help laughing.

'How do *you* think it should look?' she asked.

Gus stood up and gestured at the walls, and then at her.

'It's so *old*. It's all so old, and you're still so young. You should never have married him. He's locked you up in this middle-aged life, and you might as well be entombed.'

'But I like old things.'

'Obviously, or you couldn't have married him.'

'Touché.'

Georgiana stood up. It wasn't quite working out the way she had hoped. There was a long silence.

'Perhaps it would be better if you went back to London?'

Gus drew on his cigarette.

'Yes,' he agreed, 'perhaps it would.'

'I'm afraid I can't ring for your things,' said Georgiana, 'you'll have to fetch them yourself.'

She looked round the dining room after he had gone, seeking reassurance. The faces of her ancestors stared at her reprovingly in the candlelight. You are no better than a hoyden, they said to her. You are a chit, a romp, a fly-by-night. But how serene they looked, seemingly untroubled by the appetites that she knew they must have had. Composure was everything. Georgiana composed herself, and as she went to meet Gus in the hall it was as if he had always been going to leave at this hour. It was as if she had expected it, which she now felt she had.

Her calm disturbed him into an explanation.

'Being here with you,' he said, grinding yet another cigarette butt into the immaculate gravel, 'it makes me feel like a gigolo.'

'I understand.'

'Do you?'

'Of course. I'd feel the same if I was you.'

'Would you?'

'Of course.'

'I thought I could just be casual about you, but I can't.'

'No.'

She left off the question mark, and folded her Chinese silk shawl around her shoulders in such a way that her chin could sink into it, and only her large dark eyes stared up at him in the darkness. He put out his hand and touched her cheek with the back of it and, inevitably and at once, he was lost, for she smiled up at him mischievously, as she had always done at Kaminski, and with the same result.

'You bitch,' said Gus, and they started to make love.

In the grounds at Longborough there was a thatched cottage, a folly, somewhere where, if a grumbling Nanny could be persuaded, Georgiana would be allowed to have a tea party for her toys.

'I think it's Bink's birthday,' she would announce hopefully to Nanny, but if she was in a bad mood, Bink's birthday would become a very poor affair held behind the nursery door with only pretend food on plastic plates, and pretend drinks in cardboard cups.

Nanny however, like the gods, was not always in a bad mood, and on happy days the thatched cottage would be laid out with a real cloth, and real biscuits, and Peter Rabbit china, and the lucky toy would be feasted in style, before returning with his friends to the nursery wing, and bed in a shoe box.

Georgiana thought that the little thatched folly would be an ideal place from which Gus could paint. It meant that he could rise at his customary early hour, and while she slept, work undisturbed. She led him to the cottage through the woods. A runner of green led to the door, bordered on either side by rare wild flowers seldom seen. She told him nothing of the cottage's history as they pulled the latch and went in, Gus bending not to knock his head, for the doorway was low. She didn't trust him not to mock this little place of 'let's pretend', this thatched charm, this touchstone of happiest days of childhood.

'The light's not good enough.'

'No, I know,' said Georgiana, because she didn't at all know. 'I know, but I thought you could work *from* it, store your paints and things,' she added quickly.

'Actually that's not a bad idea,' Gus agreed, 'not a bad idea.'

'I could bring a kettle, and coffee, and little things for your use, and you could be quite quiet.'

'I'd need a day bed, or a sofa, something to lie on after lunch,' said Gus in the manner of someone ordering from a menu in a restaurant, 'and I'd like some lights in case I want to go on working in the evening.'

'We've got all those in the attics. There are some old oil lamps I've seen up there, and a horsehair sofa that used to be in the kitchen.'

Gus looked down at her.

'Well done, girl,' he said mocking her, 'well done.'

Georgiana suddenly felt terribly excited and happy. She would get brooms, and mops, and wash the windows down, and put a checked cloth on the old table in the corner, and a jug of flowers upon the cloth, and at lunchtime she would bring a covered basket down the little green path and lay out a picnic upon the table, and Gus would always be in a good mood with her, the way Nanny had sometimes been. Again she said nothing of this to Gus. He must not be allowed to know when she felt happy, or unhappy, that was not a power with which he could be entrusted.

'I'm going down to the river while you get on with it,' he announced.

From the doorway of the cottage, Georgiana watched him walking away. Once, for a short time, her father had owned a mastiff. Large, even for his breed, the dog had spent most of his time in a bed in the flower room, because he was thought to be uncertain. For the short term of his life at Longborough, Georgiana had forced him to be her friend, and on long afternoons when no one was about, she had gone to the flower room and sat between his paws, underneath his great jaw, defying him to bite her. She would sit, and he would sit, and then she would go away, quietly satisfied that he had not dared to savage her.

The furnishing of the little cottage became a pleasant occupation for Georgiana. Little forages into the long, endless attics at Longborough revealed treasures that looked wonderfully out of place in a supposedly rustic setting. And day by day, stealthily, Gus and his paints became surrounded by entirely inappropriate objects, objects that Georgiana fondly imagined would be part of her life if she was a painter's wife living in a little rustic cottage in the middle of a wood. Persian rugs were laid upon the uneven cottage floor, swathes of old materials fashioned in pretty shapes at the windows, and the oil lamps lit at dusk to greet Gus's return as the light faded. It was all very appropriately inappropriate.

Georgiana was at her most beautiful. She felt it as girls sometimes can. Summer's weather gave her white skin colour, and her slim figure bloomed and rounded in the tolerant heat. A girl and a season at the height of their beauty, but Gus ignored them both. He had discovered the river.

Georgiana loved the rustic bridge for reasons other than the water that lay almost still beneath it, and so she never went to watch him standing on it, and when he returned in the evening with paintings that did not echo what she saw, water edging its way, reeds, birds, but only echoed light and colour, she felt cheated. She was being ignored, her own charming peach tones turned from to produce the blue-grey canvases that were not recognisable reflections of the river that she knew, the trees that she had grown up with, or the rustic bridge from which she had dropped her sticks on her walk. The sleek, sinuous, full-bodied animal that she had known all her life was rivalling her, pulling her lover to its side, and the affair that they were having was not the kind of affair that she understood.

Sometimes, after lunch, with wine softening his resolution to return to work, Gus would make love to her, but it was not the kind of love-making that made him her slave, the way she wished, but the kind that leaves a man satisfied, unencumbered, ready to return to the thing that matters most, his other life, his real affair.

* * *

The sudden arrival of the Countess was in the nature of a relief. It was dramatic. It was meant to be. It was without anything but the shortest notice, a peremptory telephone call notifying that she would be at Longborough for tea, and that she would not stay longer than for a drink, as she was continuing on later to weekend somewhere else with someone else.

'Is that one of the gardeners?' she asked Georgiana as Gus strolled off into the far horizon from which he would not return until dark.

Georgiana looked at her aunt. She did not frighten Georgiana as she once had, but she frightened her enough to make it difficult to lie to her.

'No,' she said, after some thought.

'Oh it's not,' said the Countess. 'I thought not. I thought it didn't look like a gardener.' 'It' as they both knew looked just like a painter disappearing into the undergrowth.

'I hope you're not having another of your immensely unsuitable affairs, Georgiana?' said the Countess, after no pause for thought.

'More tea?'

'Yes, thank you.'

'Having affairs with unsuitable people can only amuse for so long,' said the Countess, now addressing a nearby yew tree. 'It is most important to understand that, just as it is most important to understand that women who have too many lovers, for too long, in the end and inevitably grow into Institutions. They become used, and once a woman becomes used then she's a nuisance to herself and to everyone else. She starts to regret her whole-hearted embraces, she even forgets that she has enjoyed those embraces, and she takes to blaming the opposite sex for her own follies, and once that happens there is nothing else for her to do but turn back to her diaries, and publish them in one of the cheaper Sunday newspapers. Here, in condensed form, she will be portrayed, by herself, as a hapless victim whose heart ruled her head, someone whom no one but the hardest person could really despise, not, as is always the case, a lusty, greedy person to whom restraint was foreign.'

Georgiana's foot moved slightly to avoid an early summer wasp. She was not uninterested in what the Countess had said.

She did not want to become an Institution. She did not want to end up in middle age publishing her diaries, and yet, at the same time, she did not feel that she could possibly be, as yet, eligible for the dire future that the Countess was obviously predicting for her. Two lovers was not a cricket team, and even though neither of them would be in the Countess's first eleven, on the other hand neither was negligible. They were not men whom other men could easily despise, particularly not Kaminski whom the Countess had even socialised with on a large scale, by attending his private party for five hundred.

'I think we should go and see that border your mother was describing to me the other day. She's very proud of it just now, it seems.'

She rose, and Georgiana followed her obediently.

'It is magnificent,' said the Countess, sounding surprised, because over the years there had been very few occasions on which she and Georgiana's mother had been able to find a subject upon which they could agree. 'Yes, yes, quite magnificent. Did I see it in a magazine the other day?'

'Yes, you did,' Georgiana agreed. 'They took it last year, but the colours didn't come out quite right.'

'No, but these are magnificent. Your mother's very clever.'

She stood back and straightened herself, and Georgiana, who had been feeling more than a little resentful towards her, saw that she was a little stiff, and she felt she would have liked to have taken her arm, but neither of them would have been able to cope with such a gesture, so she did not, but followed her round the garden, feeling even a little relieved when she started to grumble about the untidy way in which the gardener had pruned one of the trees.

Of course the Countess was a wonderful person. They both knew that. She was wonderful, because she had not given in to anything. They might have re-routed the motorway far too near her lovely old house, they might have taxed her income in such a way that she had been forced to take horrid ways of supplementing it, but they had not been able to either break her, or alter her vision of life. She stood for something, the past, passionate, still present.

The Countess drove on to her weekend engagement. She

drove an old but beautiful two-seater Mercedes. She drove herself. Before she drove off she put on a silk scarf, knotting the two ends behind, in the manner of film stars in the nineteen-fifties. She also donned dark glasses. She drove to the gates of Longborough, barely pausing to look for other traffic before disappearing into the exodus of Friday night. She left behind her lipstick on her teacup, a Turkish cigarette in an ashtray, and Georgiana who was restless for Gus's reappearance, and yet impatient of that restlessness. She knew that the Countess was right, but she was unable to say why it was, or what it was, that she knew that she was right about. It would be very convenient to admit that she was in love with Gus, because such an admission would be tidy, but emotional tidiness was not satisfying if the object of the admission was proving more interested in something other than herself. As always when Georgiana was dissatisfied she did the one thing that always gave her pleasure. She changed her clothes.

She laid out a white dress on her four-poster bed. It was a bright white that would be seen even if it was quite dark outside. She also laid out her gold collar, which in deference to her recent role at the rustic cottage, she had not been wearing. She thought she might do her hair in a classic style, plaited into her neck, and the thought was exciting, and made her feel creative, the way that she imagined that perhaps Gus must feel when he was painting. First however she bathed, and then she rubbed lotion all over her, and then she put on her dress. Her feet were unusual in that they were small and perfectly made. They had no disfigurements, and they looked so beautiful once she had put nail varnish on them she was obliged to admire them for a few minutes, before putting on a pair of white shoes with tall heels that supplemented her height to a satisfactory degree.

She walked through the dusk to the cottage many times in her white dress that evening, carrying the food and wine, and the glasses, and the plates. She enjoyed the thought that Gus would be returning any minute from the river, carrying his sketch books, and his paints, his head full of colour, his eyes not ready to see her yet. She would not surprise him, for she herself hated surprises, but she would force him to look at her, and earlier than he normally did.

Waiting for him was exciting.

He couldn't be surprised, because he could hear the music she was playing on the cassette player. Miles Davis' 'It Never Entered My Mind'. The lamps alight, a small fire burning, champagne, Georgiana in her white dress. To Gus it was like an Upper Class version of a Margery Allingham painting. Not sexy in the way he imagined it was meant to be, but somehow so studied, so obviously arranged, that it was touching. For the first time since the start of their affair he felt that he loved Georgiana, and was not just in love with her, and that he didn't just want to make love to her because it was laying a bit of old England, he wanted to make love to her because he saw that she was willing to please him.

'I'm afraid I'm not very good at opening wine.'

Georgiana handed him the champagne. Gus liked the way she said 'wine' for champagne. It amused him. It amused him the way his use of Cockney rhyming slang amused her, and for the same reasons. It coloured areas of themselves that might be otherwise grey, or familiar, or understandable.

He also liked her for her femininity. For instance she wouldn't even try to open the champagne, or pretend that she could, and at the same time she would apologise for the fact that she couldn't, thus encompassing all possible male attitudes. Not long after he was born Gus's mother had gone to work, because her girlfriend had and she claimed she was lonely at home; from that time his ideal woman had become someone who would wait on him, let him dominate her. It was strange that someone like Georgiana should be like this, and ironic also that she should belong to someone else.

He watched her setting out the places at the little table. Her figure held tightly into her dress. It shaped her perfectly, small-waisted and yet rounded.

'Did you do good work today?'

Gus looked at her amused. She enquired after his painting a little in the manner of someone enquiring after homework.

'I think so.'

'It was very hot today, wasn't it?'

'Yes, yes, it was.'

'My aunt came to tea.'

'Yes I saw.'

'She saw you.'

'She was meant to.'

'Why? Why was she meant to?'

'I wanted her to see me, and tell your husband. I wanted to compromise you.'

'You succeeded.'

'You're very cool.'

'What else can I be?'

Gus stood up.

'Come here.'

She stood beside him. Faintly he smelt her perfume, or 'scent' as she called it.

'Take off your shoes.'

She did so.

He lifted up her dress.

Georgiana let him. It was, after all, the reason for which she had gone to all the trouble.

The following afternoon Gus did not go to the river. He stayed in the cottage. He made love to Georgiana several times, and then started to paint her. This second painting of her he called 'Odalisque II'.

Chapter Eight

The week following Lady Tisbury's party the village was very quiet, as if there had been a street party. Few people seemed to emerge from their houses, and even fewer went for their customary walk to the shop and back. Perhaps the warmer weather meant that early tomatoes and other emergencies claimed the attentions of the inhabitants, or perhaps it was that the party had attracted the attentions of both those who had attended, and those who had not, with the consequence that those who had not remained at home for fear of bumping into those who had, and being told of an event that they would dearly have loved to have graced; or perhaps it was that those who had attended needed more time than was usual to recover from the festivities. Whichever way it was, Lady Tisbury had inadvertently wrought a change in her environment, and in a way that would have surprised her had she known, for she herself had only thought of the evening as a 'bit of fun', not a social revolution.

Margaret Paine, who was one of the great unasked, did not venture out for fear of bumping into Jane Dupont, who was one of the erratically invited. Although she knew, of course, that Jane Dupont had only been invited by dint of her collecting box, nevertheless, as she said to her husband many times that week, she was not interested in hearing *one* detail, not *one*, about the whole wretched affair, and so from Sunday to Sunday she remained firmly preoccupied by her greenhouse, which was a pity, since if she had been able to garner any details of the soirée, she would not have been uninterested.

Not that she would have learned anything from Mr Dupont, who had not only attended the soirée, but had taken part in Lady Tizzy's game with such enthusiasm that the memory of it would haunt him for the rest of his days, for he had always thought of himself as a mild sort of person, quite incapable of being swept away by the tide of events, such as had happened to him that particular night.

Nor would she have learned a great deal from Irene in the village shop, whose facility for guessing the identity of the inhabitants of her own village might have been attributed to something more than passing acquaintance. Her reaction to the dim memories of that night was to succumb to a bad attack of something mysterious, and then feel the need for a holiday on the Costa del Sol, to which she flew in great relief, leaving her father in charge of the shop, something which proved of great benefit to the village, for he was over eighty and had not mastered the decimal currency.

The only person who might have been able to capture Mrs Paine's attention with his account, and draw her away from the emergencies in her greenhouse, was Richard the window cleaner from the village. He had not actually taken part in Lady Tizzy's game, but he had witnessed it from underneath the sideboard, where he had been presumed to be asleep. Naturally, being a man to whom not a great deal had happened, despite his profession, he was most anxious to recount the exciting events of that memorable evening to anyone who would listen, and so, nightly as the yard arm slipped to the appropriate position, and the law commanded that the Queens Arms should open, he would take up an unaccustomed position at the bar and, having ordered a pint of cider, he would sit in patient wait for his fellow citizens. Unfortunately he was always too early, since most of them did not appear until he was well past his second pint of scrumpy, with the result that he never got further than 'two teams and a sheet', before whoever he was talking to would become bored, and move away, their attentions claimed by the darts board.

None of these subtleties were known to their hosts, who having done their bit in their own estimation for the 'locals', promptly went back to living life as before, to everyone's relief, but none more than poor Sir Gerard, who had privately deemed the whole thing 'hellish'.

The party from the Hall had missed most of the fun, because Jennifer, feeling unwell, had insisted on leaving early, and taking her mother and Pember with her. No one could find Andrew Gillott, so inevitably he was left to follow on, which he did at a very late hour, having not only played six rounds of Lady Tizzy's game but having fallen in love with her, so seriously that when he was forced to occupy the twin bed opposite Clarissa, who was snoring in an appalling manner, he cried himself to sleep clutching an extra pillow and imagining that it was not a piece of cotton filled with feathers, but Lady Tizzy's lovely body.

He did not feel like telling Pemberton anything the next day, because he was feeling too ill, and too lovesick, but on seeing Clarissa was intent on pursuing Jennifer round the garden for the sole purpose of criticising her rose beds, he escaped to her car and motored very slowly past the Tisburys' house in hopes of seeing the object of his new passion.

She was not to be seen and, as he sat smoking and looking at the gates to her small drive, he thought it would have been very surprising had she been there, considering that she too could not have retired to bed before half past three in the morning. Lamely he started up his car and drifted off down the little country lane, just in time to miss seeing Sir Gerard returning from a cautious hack on his old hunter.

'I'm smitten,' Andrew kept telling himself. 'I'm smitten.'

And then, having given into this most unusual of thoughts, he drove back to catch Pemberton pouring some much-needed 'stiffies'.

If love has escaped attention for many years, if the heart has not lurched unaccountably when a head is seen, or a coat, or some passing object that reminds the observer of that most miserable of states, then the impact of its arising, as it were, from nowhere, is devastating. Normally when Andrew and Pemberton drank together their conversation was a low-key exchange of racing talk and financial gossip, with perhaps a little pinch of politics if the weather played havoc and race meetings were cancelled. Today, however, Andrew could not keep to the

102

subject of his luck with a fourteen-to-one winner last week, in fact he couldn't even remember the name of the horse that had won for him, and he appeared to have total amnesia as far as the City and so on went, for even as he pretended to respond to Pemberton he could only hear Lady Tizzy's divine voice, and see Lady Tizzy's divine form. It was quite dreadful, and after lunch he was forced to excuse himself and go and lie down.

Once more upon his bed, the pillow cradled into his arms, he imagined that it was her, and slept to be awoken by the voice of his own true wife, a sound as welcome as the early bell had been at St Peter's Prep for the utterly wretched sons of gentlemen.

'Andrew, you simply cannot go on snoring all afternoon, it's very bad for you, and rude to Jennifer, you must come down to tea, and then take a turn or two in the garden.'

Clarissa was wearing a brown checked dress such as she much favoured at the moment, and sandals with a thick wedge heel. Lady Tizzy, Andrew had no doubt, would even now be slipping into something silky, shimmering and diaphanous, and pulling on a pair of startlingly high stiletto heels, such as she had sported last night. He half closed his eyes imagining to himself that it was she who was standing before him, and not the hateful Clarissa, his soon-to-be-got-rid-of wife.

'I'm too ill,' he said.

'You weren't too ill to stay out late last night, so you can't be too ill to come down to tea.'

Clarissa turned on her wedge heel and left the room before Andrew could think of a suitable reply to this latest piece of matronly logic. Life with Clarissa was so unspeakable that he felt that if it did not end soon he would cut his throat; and then suddenly, last night, just as he had evaded the first half of the party by wandering round the garden with his hip flask, and then falling comfortably asleep in the stables, just as he had done that, and emerged with hay in his hair and all over his evening jacket, he had heard Lady Tizzy laughing, and then he had seen her standing in the garden, her magnificent poitrine bumping up and down with gentle giggles, her stunning figure, her wonderfully lipsticked mouth, her festoon of hair spun out to tease and provoke every man who passed her so that he would have to suppress a desire to ruffle it –

at that moment he had fallen in love, hopelessly, and for the time being, forever.

Even now as he thought about it he groaned out aloud, so that Clarissa, who was halfway to the main staircase heard him and hurried back to enquire whether she should fetch a doctor? But Andrew had read his Shakespeare, and he knew that there was no doctor that could take this pain from him, only a surgeon could cut it out; so he pretended to be brave, and told the Mu-Mu Maiden that he would be down in a minute.

'If you're absolutely sure?' asked Clarissa anxiously, for having achieved the status of the Honourable Mrs Gillott after a long period of widowhood, she was loath to resume her weeds again in too great a hurry.

'Quite sure, quite sure. Leave me, and I will join you in a minute.'

He swung his legs to the side of the bed, and sat upright. His life had changed overnight. Now he actually wanted to live in the country. In fact he couldn't wait to move into the house that Clarissa had bought for them both, as it was only a few miles from Lady Tizzy. He would be able to pass by her gates every day if he wanted to, and occasionally if the Knight, her husband, was out, Andrew could call and leave her flowers.

He walked to the looking glass and stared at himself. An older man looked out at him, somewhat grey, somewhat ill-kempt, but not wholly without dignity. He would slim, he would give up drink, he would give up smoking, and the new person that would undoubtedly emerge would be a man of dignity, a man worth all that he would have to ask Lady Tizzy to give up for him, for she surely couldn't stay married to Sir Gerard for one minute once Andrew had declared his love to her; but before that happened stringent reforms were needed, dieting, walking, exercises, recommendations he normally skipped over in the papers came floating up to him as he walked downstairs to tea. He had a vague feeling that there was going to be a lot of celery needed, and yoghurt, and something disgusting called Slimwit that Clarissa put in her coffee.

Out on the lawn the ladies sat. Each staring at a different part of the garden while they directed their observations at each other, rather than to each other, as women will, when one or two are gathered together. Jennifer was busy sticking her stomach out a little to pronouncedly, because she knew it annoyed her mother. Her mother did not like pregnancy. Pregnancy was a token of your having done something that ladies did not do. It also meant you were fertile, which reminded Clarissa that she was not.

'Andrew, what are you doing?'

Clarissa's voice floated sharply across the lawn. 'What *are* you doing?' she repeated.

'Helping myself to tea with lemon,' said Andrew with dignity.

'Tea with lemon? But you never have tea with lemon. He never has tea with lemon.'

By now the whole estate must know that Andrew Gillott never had tea with lemon.

'Well, I'm having it now.'

'You must be feeling ill, you poor darling.'

The poor darling lowered himself into a deck chair, and stared at the piece of lemon floating in his cup of tea, and then he raised the cup slowly to his lips, and sipped. It was sharp, it was a little scented, not what he was used to, but not unpleasant. As he sipped he raised his eyes and stared triumphantly over the top of his teacup at Clarissa. She did not know what he knew. She would not know, not until the very last minute, just before he left her. And when he did leave her, he would be a slim youngish man with a well-kept appearance, no longer the butt of jokes at the Claremont. He was going to be the kind of man that his mother would have wanted him to be, not a middle-aged drunk that had been reduced to marrying a woman from the middle class seeking to raise her status. And although rising from a deck chair was now an effort, in a few weeks it would no longer be.

'Where are you going?' called Clarissa, as he started to walk down the lawn to the orchard.

'I'm going to walk as you told me to,' said Andrew.

'He can't be at all well,' said Clarissa brushing a little crumb of sponge from the front of her dress. 'It's not like him to walk anywhere.'

Jennifer closed her eyes and stroked her stomach gently. It was very soothing. She had taught Pember how to do it during her last pregnancy, little butterfly strokes that seemed to cool the stretched skin. Pember did not seem too keen to do it during this pregnancy, and this disappointed Jennifer, for he had been so attentive before. Probably getting blasé about it all, thought Jennifer dreamily. Or perhaps it just didn't interest him anymore, didn't hold the same thrill. Whatever the reason, she meant to jolt him out of his apathy. She would go away for a little while, and not telephone him when he expected her to, or she would go to London and spend a great deal of money and make him anxious that way.

On seeing Andrew walking in the orchard, Pemberton hid. He wanted to be alone, and the sight of Andrew striding purposefully through the grass was vaguely upsetting. He did not want to be roused from his Sunday afternoon fantasies by Andrew. He wanted to remain in a soft sleepy mood, a mood that would allow him to dream about leading another kind of life, one that would encompass someone more lively than Jennifer, someone who would wear daring clothes, leather skirts, and fantasy stilettos. The feeling of unrest that had overwhelmed him in the early hours had now turned to a containable, pleasant form of desire. He throbbed a little when he thought of someone, someone who lived not a great distance from him who wore such things.

Hidden from Andrew, his back against a tree, he knew he had not had this pleasant craving since he was a little boy. It was not love, it was not passion, it was just a little excitement, just a little naughty feeling that no doubt would pass, meaning nothing to anyone but him, but nevertheless it was very pleasant and he did not want it to go.

'Andrew!'

The old trees seemed to cover their ears at the sound of Clarissa's harsh voice.

'Andrew!'

The sound now took on a persecuting insistence, a feeling that should Andrew not answer soon she herself would not be answerable for the consequences. Pemberton saw Andrew hiding. The voice continued, and then stopped and went away.

The sun began to grow bored of its summer task, and as the light became eclipsed by busy evening clouds and mosquitoes crowded, the two men remained in place, hiding.

Naturally Patti was unaware of any stir that she might have made in the County. Coming from a profession where youth and beauty were in their way as commonplace as the opposite in Wiltshire, she did not notice male appreciation any more than she noticed that she was breathing. She was not an introvert, but she did sometimes wonder what she would find to do in the country in the coming winter. She knew that Knightey had quite set his heart upon the idea that she would be riding side by side with him in the hunting field, but this idea had little or no appeal to Patti, whose idea of what to do on a winter's day was to go shopping and spend money, and then go home and be taken out to dinner.

She had heard people talking all summer of mysterious occupations such as 'coursing' and 'shooting lunches', and although she thought she knew what they were, on the other hand she also thought that she would rather not know, because they all sounded really rather non-vegetarian, and while she was not a dedicated card-holding Vegan, nevertheless she did draw the line at doing all the killing yourself.

Sometimes when she lay in bed in the mornings, while Knightey was out riding and she was meant to be exercising Havoc in preparation for this exciting time in the hunting field, sometimes she felt tempted to feel sorry for herself. It was not that she did not love Knightey, for of course she did, and she knew he loved her, that was quite evident, but she did not like the same things as Knightey liked, now that he was living in the country again. In town they had got along so very well, because they both liked going to Mark's Club, and the shops and everything, but now he was back in his native habitat they did not always seem to want to sing the same song.

Of course she did not like to admit how much they had stopped sharing, for such admissions might lead her to make decisions, and decisions were all together too decisive for Patti who had managed to achieve twenty-seven without having to force too many upon herself. Nevertheless she recognised that not exercising Havoc was not the answer, accomplished though she had become at it, even down to rubbing a little mud on him, in case he looked too clean.

The deception did not make her feel bad because as long as Knightey was happily out riding thinking that she was happily out doing the same, she really couldn't see what harm she could be doing? Not only that but it was much kinder to the poor old horse to keep him in, and not put all those dreadful things into his mouth, and make him carry her up and down the hill. In fact she quite enjoyed the whole exercise. Rising early with the lark while Knightey was plunging about finding all his riding clothes. Climbing into her excellently tailored jodhpurs, polishing her boots with tender care, waving happily to her best beloved as he rode off to wherever he was going, and then turning smartly round, removing her boots, splashing them a little in a puddle, and going straight back to bed with a cup of coffee and a magazine. It was really quite enjoyable, but what wasn't enjoyable was the thought of what was going to happen next. What was going to happen when she had to confront Knightey and tell him that she couldn't face flying over hedges and ditches on the back of an animal that was well down the line when they handed out brains? Nothing very nice, it seemed, but whatever happened it couldn't be as bad as what would happen if she went out hunting, of that she was quite sure.

Summer had slipped on and already she felt that it would soon be time to go shopping for autumn clothes, but this particular morning it was decidedly too warm to be tempted to go back to bed. Besides, she had the feeling that she had slept too much lately. Instead she dressed herself and tiptoed into the garden with her cup of coffee to sit under the old yew tree and admire the fact that she had a garden.

Needless to say she had hardly sat down when the old-fashioned bell rang from inside the cellar, and she, because she had no daily on Tuesdays, had to struggle out of her temporary content and go to answer it.

It was Pemberton. He was wearing a tweed cap, a tall handsome sight if you liked that kind of look, which personally nowadays Patti did not. Personally, in fact, she felt that if she saw one more person in a green loden anything, or one more cap in a tweedy mix, she would be tempted to scream. But that was quite beside the point, since Pemberton was the Seventh Marquis of whatever, even she knew that it was not appropriate to scream, just because he happened to be wearing a tweed cap and knickerbockers with green socks. Anyway, he was now removing his cap, to reveal a good head of hair and a perfectly polished complexion.

'Good morning, Lady T.'

Although she had been married for nearly three years Patti still found herself half tempted to look behind her when people addressed her as Lady Tisbury.

'Good morning John,' she said, a little curt, because her heart was still with her cup of coffee under the tree, even if he was the Seventh Marquis and not a milkman, calling on her.

There was a small silence during which Pemberton breathed in the clean morning air, and the sight of Lady Tizzy barefooted, tumble-haired and sporting a leather mini skirt and angora jumper which fluffed up around her prow like an adorable new-born chick. Her scent too was delicious. Again that lovely feeling crept over him, warm like a bath, soft like her jumper. He would have liked to have stroked her, but he did not think it would be understood.

'Yard's coming on.'

He nodded towards the new outbuildings that Knightey had spent a fortune putting up.

'May I see?'

Patti walked carefully barefoot over the stones to the yard. He walked behind her. It was a wonderful sight.

'Fine boxes, very fine. Good yard, well designed,' said Pemberton looking round.

Patti thought it looked fairly frightful, but since everyone kept saying the same thing about Knightey's stables, she supposed she had to believe him. The annoying thing was that in the country everyone stood in the stable block and asked questions, but when they went inside the house they didn't take the slightest notice of all her nice furnishings, but went straight to the drinks table, and stayed there talking about, of all things, the wretched stables.

She took Pemberton back into the house, because she

couldn't think of anything else to do with him, and then reluctantly she showed him into the garden, to her private place under the tree, and brought him a cup of coffee, which he only made a small show of trying to refuse.

She sat down beside him. It was the first time they'd ever been alone, and she was very apprehensive about what to talk about, so used was she to Knightey always being there to cover up for her.

'I thought you might be out riding,' he said, 'you know, because Havoc wasn't in his box. So used to seeing the old fellow's head popping out over the top of his box when you drive up.'

Patti looked up at him. She couldn't believe it. Horses for breakfast, horses for coffee, horses, horses, horses, did anyone ever talk about anything else in the country? Or to put it another way, what on earth would they find to talk about if they didn't have horses?

'Knightey took Havoc out because Percy's hurt his foot, I think. Something like that.'

'Hoof.'

'Sorry?'

'Something to do with his hoof,' said Pemberton kindly.

He pronounced it 'huff', which made Patti feel in one.

'His front foot,' said Patti, refusing to be converted to his terminology.

Pemberton smiled. It was really rather endearing the way she was so useless at talking about horses. It made him want to stroke her more, and tell her all the points of the horse.

'More coffee?'

'Yes. It's very good. Must get Jennifer to find out how you do it, her coffee tastes like something on British Rail. Talking of which, which we weren't, wondered whether Gerard and you, that is, wondered whether you'd like to come over and dine with us tomorrow night? Just the four of us, nothing very special. You know. Her ladyship's condition being what it is, she's not much in the mood for entertaining a large number. You know how it is.'

'Yes,' said Patti, who didn't in the least.

'I expect the food will be frightful as usual but there's nothing much I can do about that until Bloss gets back from his week off.'

110

My wife is many things, but caterer and cook she is not.'

Pemberton smiled to take the little unkindness that lay beneath this statement out of his words, and then he finished his coffee, and stood up.

'Shall we take a tour around the garden?' he asked. 'You might like to point out a few plants to me.'

Patti remained seated. She would not like to point out anything to Pemberton, and for the very good reason that she had not an idea of what, or which, might be growing in the whole place.

'I'm not very good at plants,' she said.

Pemberton smiled.

'Don't worry, I am.'

It was really just an exercise to get her walking in front of him in that mini skirt again, and seeing those fabulously naked legs move gracefully over the grass, beckoning back that lovely warm feeling that he so enjoyed.

'Oh goodness, what's this then?' asked Patti bending down innocently.

'I've no idea,' said Pemberton, not looking.

Patti turned round, and then she went to sit down. She wasn't that stupid.

Pemberton sighed. He had been caught out in his little enjoyment, and it made him blush.

'Naughty man,' Patti murmured.

He sat down, and more to fill the silence than anything else, Patti told him about her dread of going hunting, and how it was that she had been busy deceiving Knightey by pretending to ride Havoc when he was out, but how she had been too frightened and had just pretended to ride the poor horse, because she was both too scared to confess her fear, and too scared to get on the horse.

'Naughty puss,' said Pemberton.

Then after a minute or two something occurred to him.

'But hasn't Gerard been feeding Havoc up to go cubbing?'

'He always feeds him.'

'No. What I mean is – hasn't he been feeding him *up*.'

'I don't know what you mean?'

'Here's how it is. To take Havoc out hunting, or cubbing,

you've got to get him fit, well no, not cubbing, hunting, a horse has to be fit, same as a man, you see?'

Patti quite obviously didn't.

'Same as you? You want to dance, you have to eat up your oats and get fit? Well, that's what happens to horses. You feed 'em up, get 'em fit, and take 'em out in the field.'

'And then what happens?'

'And then what happens? Then what happens is that they go like the clappers until it's time to stop.'

He laughed.

Pemberton had stopped laughing when the doorbell rang again. This time Patti rose with alacrity. She didn't know why, but she was rather regretting telling Pemberton about riding Havoc. She didn't think she should. She had been unfaithful telling him something that she should already have told Knightey. Not that she thought Pemberton would tell Knightey, but you could never be sure. And not being sure, it really meant that she would now have to tell Knightey herself. She imagined how she would do it as she went to the door.

'You know about the hunting, Knightey darling?' she would say, 'Well I'd really rather not, if you don't mind?'

And then when he was busy getting angry she would give him a wonderful dinner, and a wonderful time afterwards, and everything would be wonderful after all.

She padded into the hall. A man in a green, country green jacket, much too hot for this weather obviously, for he was panting, stood in the doorway, beyond the glass of the doors. She could see him quite clearly. She saw his face. She saw how hot he was, and she wondered why he was dressed too warmly for the day and why he was breathing so heavily? And then she saw his eyes, and she knew that she would not be able to hear his words, because Knightey, her Knightey, was dead, and those words that she had been saving up, and that dinner that she had been planning, and that wonderful time that she was going to give him, they would not be going to happen, not tonight, nor any other night, and nothing nice was going to happen to her again for a very long time.

'I don't believe you,' she said, before the man even spoke.

*   *   *

Whenever Pemberton looked back to that particular morning in early autumn, which he never did with anything but great reluctance, it seemed to him that he was being punished. That his mother had sent poor Gerard out on that wretched horse, that she, the wicked witch from S.W.1., had somehow known of his enjoyment of that morning, of Lady Tizzy's remarkable charms, of being a man, and had caused Havoc to rear up on the road, and kill the poor man. Undoubtedly, of course, the guilt of it all had caused him worse suffering than the business of Sir Gerard's demise, because no one could have died a happier man than he, of that everyone was sure. To be on his horse one minute, and then in the arms of his maker the next, was what he would have planned for himself, and amidst all the shock of the news there was undoubtedly a feeling in the village, and in the Hunt, that he could not have exited more perfectly to the great hunting field in the sky. And what's more he had died like a gentleman should, wearing a bowler and not one of these silly modern things made out of reinforced concrete.

The wreaths at the funeral naturally reflected this. There were quite a few 'gorn aways' from the less tasteful, and other vulgarities, which made the Countess sigh rather loudly.

No one quite knew why the Countess was present, except that she always did seem to be present at funerals, and her name was so often reflected in the columns of *The Times* that a number of less kind people had become convinced that she was being paid for her services, for there was no doubt about it but that a Countess at the top of a list of 'those present' added tone to even the most attended funeral.

'At least the wreaths from his first marriage have a great deal more taste than the others,' she said to Andrew Gillott.

Andrew, who was longing to support the widow on his own arm, and was feeling suffocatingly jealous over the fact that Pemberton seemed to have been doing so ever since the poor Knight had been flung on the road, wasn't paying much attention to the wreaths.

'What do you think of the new posy shape for wreaths?' asked the Countess.

Andrew could think of nothing but how beautiful Patti looked in her grey silk suit, so he did not reply but went behind a gravestone to take a sip or ten from his hip flask, because now that Lady Tizzy was a widow, now that she was free, all his good resolutions to become slimmer and trimmer had flown out of the window in the excitement, and he had returned to his bad old ways; except now he knew that it would be for only a few days, just until he could recover from this dreadful euphoria that he had been feeling ever since Sir Gerard's death. It was terrible to be so pleased that the poor chap had passed away, but fair was fair, and there was no doubt about it the noble Knight had had at least three glorious years with Lady Tizzy, and it was only parity that he should now go to the Master in the sky and let someone else have a go of her.

'The widow goes beautifully with everything,' said the Countess graciously, 'very fetching.'

'Yes, she looks lovely,' agreed Lady Mary. 'Grey suits her. And I thought the service was very well done, didn't you, Hugo?'

'Beautifully done,' agreed Hugo, squinting at one of the engravings on a neighbouring stone.

'John chose the service,' said the Countess with satisfaction.

'I thought it had the hand of a fine mind,' said Hugo.

'You don't know what you're talking about,' said the Countess.

'No,' agreed Hugo, 'I wasn't really thinking.'

'No.'

The Countess looked at Mary.

'What do you think of the posy shape, the new posy shape?' she asked.

'I like it,' said Lady Mary, 'I like it. Much neater.'

'Yes, I like it,' agreed the Countess, making it official. 'Of course those horse shoes, all those ones, are from the other side of the family.'

They started to walk towards their waiting cars.

'What do you think is going to happen?' asked the Countess. 'I mean what's going to happen to her? He must have left most of his money to his children, since it was his first wife's anyway, and she can't remain here, in the country, she doesn't fit in.'

'No, she doesn't fit in,' agreed Lady Mary. 'But why wouldn't he have left her any money?'

114

'They never do,' said the Countess. 'Feel too guilty. You know how it is. Children never approve of their parents enjoying themselves, so the parents, if they manage to enjoy themselves before they go, they feel they must make it up to the children afterwards.'

'Yes, but he would have left her the house, surely?'

The Countess yawned as her driver opened the door.

'I shall be very surprised if he has, very surprised. Do you want to come with me?'

'No, I'm going with Hugo,' said Lady Mary.

'Oh very well, see you up at the house.'

Lady Mary sighed as she watched her mother being driven away. She was tiresome, so she was always finding everyone else tiresome, as tiresome as anything, but she was hardly going to stop being so now, and the sooner that Mary became used to that thought the better. She turned to look at Hugo. He was studying himself in the reflection of the car window. She smiled slightly. She sometimes thought he only ever gazed into her eyes to see how his hair looked.

Bloss opened the door to the returning funeral party with the gravitas suitable to the occasion. He had been able to hire extra staff for the occasion, something which he very much enjoyed, and he had been able to lay out the dining table with all four leaves, which was something else that he enjoyed. It was a melancholy fact that Lady Pemberton was so uninterested nowadays in entertaining of any kind, that it took a funeral to brighten up the place.

Heaven knows, like his routine as he might, there were only so many ways you could present dinner, or lunch, for two.

There were an odd mixture of people present at the funeral party. The Knight Errant's relations from his first marriage did not dare to show their true feelings towards the widow since she was in the Hall, and supported on both sides by men of a more distinguished line than their own. Nevertheless they did not stay long enough to give anyone the idea that they were anything but embarrassed by this last remains, however beautiful, of an old man's lust.

Jennifer was not altogether happy that Patti had managed to look so lovely. It did not seem quite proper somehow.

However, she had to be grateful to Patti for providing the County with such drama and excitement. First of all there had been the accident, and the whole business of Patti wanting to shoot the horse, her hysteria, and then the funeral, and now soon would be the will, and more excitement. It had kept Nanny and her going for the past week, and no doubt would be so doing for some future weeks.

Frankly Jennifer would have liked to have felt a little sorry for Patti but, young as she was to be widowed, she really could not, for if you marry a man so much older you must know that at one time or another he would be more than likely to cross the line into the next world, and leave you with a will and new avenues to explore, although what avenues those were would, of course, depend very much on the will. That it had happened to Patti to be widowed was not surprising, *how* it had happened was surprising.

Pemberton was being dreadfully noble, which was perfectly all right, for the moment. Supporting the widow in the fortnight following the demise was entirely understandable, but more than that would raise eyebrows, and the moment she could take him to Norfolk, for a change of air, there was no doubt that she would, because whichever way you looked at it, sooner or later – and Jennifer was determined to make it sooner – Patti was going to have to fend for herself.

Clarissa sidled up to Jennifer as the first wife's relations were departing.

'I wonder how he's left things?'

'I thought the service was awfully well done, didn't you?' asked Jennifer.

'I mean, I believe it was the first wife who had the money, and she spent most of it on trying to improve hounds, or something ghastly, and that she left it to him, or the income of it to him, but in trust to the children, or something. So the chances are that she won't be able to get her greedy little hands on any of it. That's what I believe.'

'Pember chose the hymns. Don't you think they were well done?'

Jennifer moved away from her mother, but her mother followed her quite unable to resist feeding her further information, and quite unimpressed by her efforts to ignore her.

'It's always dreadful, isn't it? When they marry some old man in the hopes of inheriting, and then it all goes to the children. Such a disappointment, and after all they've had to put up with.'

'I'm sure you're wrong.'

'I'm quite sure *you're* wrong dear, quite sure. They'll do everything they can to ruin her. And more, if it is possible!'

Clarissa laughed.

Jennifer looked over to where Pember was standing. He was some ten years older than her, but now they had been married for a little while it sometimes seemed to her, particularly when he was with other people, that she was much older than him. She often wondered whether it wasn't always so with men and women. Women born old, men born young, in their minds anyway.

She sat down. Her feet were tired from the pregnancy, and from the excitement, of one kind or another. Her mother too sat down, and very near her. Jennifer closed her eyes momentarily. She really just wanted to sit and watch Charles playing with his toys. She didn't really like grown-ups and their wills, and men and women, just the sweet cuddly results of men and women. And Nanny. She really loved Nanny. Sometimes it seemed she was as much Jennifer's nanny as Charles's.

'Now then, Lady P., in you get,' Nanny would say, stirring the bathwater round, and then discreetly turning her back as Jennifer climbed in. 'Not too hot in your condition.'

Just so long as she went on having babies Nanny would go on staying with her, and as long as Nanny went on staying with her, and the nursery was full, then that would be as long as Jennifer would be happy.

The plan was for Patti to spend the night at the Hall, and then return to Flint House where her own relations were staying, and a right motley crowd they looked, thought Fulton delightedly, as they all fell into the food and drink as if they hadn't been fed since last Christmas. He felt sorry for poor Lady Tizzy, having her relations turn up like that meant that there would be very little hope for her future just as long as they were around. Of course it was nobody's fault where they came from, and everyone knew that no one could be blamed for their relations, and that was a fact and stale news too, but nevertheless, even given a wet sail and the wind in the right direction, where Lady Tizzy's lot had blown in from, heaven, and only heaven, would know.

'This is very larky for a funeral,' said Elliott, 'I must say.'

Fulton frowned. Elliott was going too far, even if it was true.

'You know we're going to have to look after Lady Tizzy, now?'

'Of course.'

'We're going to have to be the good fairies at the funeral. Widows need to be surrounded by wild flowers until they get on their feet, and find someone else.'

'Hoity-toity hark at you.'

'Elliott, I am très serious, really.'

'Fulton, I know. I can see by your deadly earnest expression. Any time you start looking like boiled cod, I know I'm in for a lecture.'

'You know the poor old sod hasn't finished paying our bill?'

'WHAT?'

'No, I know. Let's hope he's changed his will, because the rumour is that it's all in trust to those rather unattractive looking children of his.'

'Oh well, tempis, it's only merney.'

'Quite. Oh dear, look at Patti's mother – she's doing something horrible –'

Elliott closed his eyes tightly.

'Coward.'

'She sneezed! She only sneezed.'

'Don't. That's bad enough.'

'Is the rumour that he fell off his horse and then went to heaven? Or did he go to heaven and then fall off his horse, if you know what I mean?'

'I think he had a heart attack thing, and then fell off his horse.'

'I heard it threw him.'

'Whatever – he has gorn away – and now we must be the sole support of Patti.'

'J'arrive.'

They moved away from the champagne, and into the thick of the revelling mourners.

* * *

118

As predicted, the will was not good for Patti. To do her credit she had never thought of asking Knightey about his will, or enquiring as to whether or not it was in her favour, or anything else of that nature. She had merely met an older man whom she had thought of as something very special, which indeed he was in her world.

'Only a silly cow like Patti *wouldn't* get him to alter his will,' said Fulton, almost affectionately, when he heard.

But Patti had been too grateful to look to the future. Knightey had taken her away from being a waitress at night, and an already ageing dancer trudging the streets from audition to audition by day. He had also given her something else. A lifestyle, a bit of class, and that bit of class that had given her a bit of class had gone, and she was quite alone.

The house would have to go. That she did not regret a great deal, for on her own she felt it to be a strange place. It had few things that were 'her' in it, and even less with which she felt at home. The rooms were purposeless without the big G, so she would stay as long as she could in the garden, which was anonymous compared to the house.

The house went on the market, and as soon as it appeared in the estate agent's window, it became imperative for the people living within driving distance, all of whom had no intention of moving, to be shown around; but even that task, in her loneliness, was pleasurable, compared to being alone and trying to think. Every so often she would find herself by a lake in a wood nearby, and she would sit, barefooted, staring across the water, watching the horizon as if she expected Sir Gerard to arrive in a little rowing boat at any minute to collect her.

Being alone was a new experience for her. Not to expect anyone was strange. She had not the habit of it, for she had grown up surrounded by aunts and cousins, in a household of many and varying relationships, where to be on your own was a cause for commiseration, and now this state of isolation could not make her feel optimistic. Living with Knightey had changed her. It had changed her faster than she had realised, and when she had seen her family at the funeral she knew that she could never return to them. She had not been ashamed of them, but she had not been proud of them. They did not really like her any more, because she 'associated', as they put it, with people they did not understand. The sort of people they did not know themselves, and now it seemed they looked on her as 'one of those people', and they were right, for she too now looked on herself as 'one of those people', even if 'those people' knew that she was not 'one of them', and never would be.

Nowadays she did not like nylon sheets, or tea at six. She did not like sharing her bathwater, or tinned food. At first she had not liked these things because she had been told by Gerard not to like them, but now she disliked them because she no longer liked them. She was unfortunate. A chicken who had learned to swim with the ducks, only to be returned to the farmyard once more. Happily she knew that feeling sorry for yourself was ageing, or she might feel like giving way to self-pity, but vanity, as always, was a saving grace, and so she hummed 'Pretty Polly Perkins' a little tunelessly to herself to drown her sad thoughts. Something would happen. It always did.

Chapter Nine

Gus had returned to London, leaving Georgiana in supreme control of her own house, or what she thought of as her own house. He had returned to London with several paintings of her, but nothing to match the beauty of 'Odalisque II', which he himself admitted was one of his best paintings. He left her with great reluctance. He had finally become almost possessive about her in the last days that he had been at Longborough, and consequently Georgiana was a little glad to see him go; also she looked forward to measuring the amount that she missed him once he was gone.

In another way too, it gave her a little time to restore herself physically. To sleep in the mornings, after a light breakfast, to rub away any hard skin that she imagined might have accrued on her elbows, to tidy up her eyebrows, and altogether to do any little jobs that might have lapsed while she was maintaining someone other than herself. To be beautiful was a way of life, and it was a way of life that she knew she could never abandon.

She was beautiful until her parents arrived back from holiday, and then she was just Georgiana again. Georgiana might look beautiful to everyone else, but to her parents she was the girl who wasn't the boy, the child of little interest, and now the young woman who irritated.

She found she still parked her car in the wrong place, that she didn't have enough friends, except when they came to stay when she had too many friends. She had had a famous lover who had lavished money on her, which was vulgar, and yet she had not made a good marriage. When Georgiana went to visit them to ask after their holiday she was not the model for 'Odalisque II', but a person after whom her parents would not ask unless asked. And if they did address a question to her it was usually not the one to which they required an answer, with the consequence that the three of them seldom, if ever, found out anything about each other, except through a third party.

It was not therefore surprising that Georgiana only discovered the financial straits that were again upon them through Nanny.

'It's too big for them Lady Georgie, much too big.'

'How do you mean? Do you mean their apartment, their flat's too big for them?'

'The whole place. The whole place's too big for them.'

'But they don't live in the whole place. I've made it so that they don't have to live in it all.'

'No, Lady Georgie, no, that's not the point. The point is that they can feel the rest of the place round them, half empty, and they don't like it.'

'*You* can't say it's too big now Nanny, can you?'

Nanny ignored this.

'They're not as young as they were. They want something more convenient.'

'But I've made it convenient for them. They wanted two floors. That's what they said they wanted.'

'And then there's the gardener. He's not enough. He doesn't do enough to help your father. And there's no point in you looking like that, Lady Georgie, no point at all. It's about time you grew up, Lady Georgie. Your parents aren't getting any younger. And they don't want to get any younger, and since you haven't married, they don't want to stay here. They want to sell it, and it's theirs to sell if they should so wish, and I think you should let them do it, I think that's the very least you can do, since you're obviously not going to get married.'

Georgiana left her. She couldn't stand any more of the stupid woman rattling on. Knowing Nanny she'd probably find she was at the bottom of it all. Probably find she was fed up with dusting the newel posts, or didn't like taking Harry his tea in the garden, or something. Nannies were old goats, but old goats could still butt you.

She ran down the green path to the rustic cottage, which she now thought of as Gus's studio, and she sat there until it was too dark not to feel cold and damp, because that was how she felt inside. She knew what they were doing to her, she knew that they were threatening her. What they were really saying was that she must do as she was told, get married or sell Longborough. She might not be a boy, she might not be anything but a nuisance, but that it seemed was the least they were owed for not loving her. She must come to heel or she would be left alone and palely loitering, a single girl in a city of single girls.

'It's so unfair, it's so unfair,' she said in the darkness, and from the darkness came the reply that she knew was always waiting.

'But life's not fair, Lady Georgie. If life was fair, naughty little girls like you would not be born in nice houses with warm clothes, and nice things to eat, they would be born in slums with rats running over them, and no nice clothes to wear. And nice girls would be born like you in nice houses with lots of food in their tummies. But that's not how it is, is it? That's why it's just as well life's not fair, isn't it Lady Georgie, or you'd be with the rats, wouldn't you? Now eat up.'

She had always been a naughty girl. From the moment she had been born a girl. Born naughty meant being born a girl. She was the last of a long line, and the long line would die with her, but if it had Longborough still, something would be left alive, because Longborough was 'it', the something that made you different. The place where you came from. The house that said that you might be nothing to everyone else, but you were something to it.

Other Lady Georgies had run down that little green path, other naughty children had thrown their beastly food from Longborough's windows. They had laughed and loved and been laid to rest there, and when she was alone she felt them round her, touching her, whispering to her, telling her that she was only as naughty as they had been, and she felt their sweetness. She must do something for them, for her, for all of them. She must stop being able to be punished.

She didn't return to the house that evening, because she couldn't face any of the questions it would ask her, and so instead she took her Chinese shawl from the back of the chair where Gus had liked to sit as the light faded, and she wrapped it round herself, and lay down on the studio bed, and stayed awake, knowing what she must do, and yet not wanting to know. The sounds of the night, the hunting owl, the sudden cry of death, they were all compatible with what she knew lay out there for her. She had told Gus that 'they' would always win, and so, it seemed, it appeared, they would.

In the morning she slept in, putting off the moment when she would return to the house, and lay out her clothes for London, preparing for what had to be done. Eventually it would no longer be delayed, and she shook out her shawl and laid it decoratively over the chair, then, shoes in hand, as if she was returning from some midsummer ball, she walked up to the house and let herself into the apartment.

All traces of 'Lord Longborough' had been removed days before and returned to her parents, and now there was only herself to be seen in evidence. The luxuries of her possessions restored her a little. She was too neat, but each item, each possession – scent, stockings, silk underwear – each was perfectly kept, perfectly arranged when she took it off, so that even in its inert state it made a picture.

Gus would mock her.

'It's all so *House and Garden*,' he would declaim from her White House sheets. 'Can't you do anything imperfectly?'

She didn't know what he meant.

'Ruffle yourself, woman. Become a human being. Join the human race. Have a weakness!'

She thought he was being silly, and knew that he was not, and yet she had no idea of what he was talking, just as she had no idea of how 'human beings', as he called them constantly, went on. Did he mean that she should not want everything to be perfect? And if he did, well, that was insupportable. You had to be perfect in everything you did, because you were so imperfect. Life could not be permitted to be otherwise.

'I sometimes think your heart would stop if your clothes were untidy,' he said once.

Georgiana didn't reply, but secretly she thought it might.

'You'd never make a bloody painter. You couldn't bear to get your brushes dirty.'

124

'I don't understand. Why don't you like things to be beautiful?'

'Your idea of beauty, Lady Longborough, is not my idea of beauty. Your idea of beauty is pure magazine fiction. You should grow up, look at life as it is, see the beauty on the rubbish tip.'

Georgiana shuddered. She had once actually gone to a tip. The birds circling above, the remnants of a plastic civilisation, the frightful smell that the objects had decided would be their common-law odour, it had been terrible. She thought Gus was mad, but she didn't tell him so, she hated to annoy him, for if she annoyed him he would stop painting her.

She loved to hear him talk, even though she couldn't understand half the things he told her. He talked to her about the theory of colour, and of the painters that had influenced him. Sometimes he told her about the lives of other painters. She liked to hear about Renoir, of men who loved to paint the women they loved. She liked happy stories. Others she didn't like, and she tried to rearrange them.

'But couldn't he have painted things to sell, and then painted what he wanted at the weekends?'

'No, he could not.'

'But why? Why couldn't he?'

'Because he wasn't like that. Because he didn't want to do that kind of work.'

'But his poor wife? And the poor children? Couldn't he have thought of them?'

'You're such a little philistine. You'll never understand. Just lie back and be beautiful, it's all you're good at.'

Now there was going to have to be another unhappy ending, and she did not know how to face it. Of course she knew that love affairs have to end in something, and that something was either another love affair, or a marriage; but even so, knowing how little she knew Gus, she understood that it was going to be difficult.

'Lord Longborough' was going to have to find out, of course, and that would be unsurprising, since the Countess had seen Gus and since he had meant her to see him, but the fact that he had been so deliberate in his lack of concealment made

Georgiana uneasy. Before Georgiana could do what she had to do, she thought she would visit the Countess.

Andrew Gillott was there. He had come up to London to enable Clarissa to spend a great deal of time at Peter Jones choosing all the wrong lampshades, and quite a few of the wrong curtain materials.

'I'm drowning in Dralon,' he groaned to the Countess.

The Countess nodded approvingly.

'Sit down, silly fellow, and have a gin.'

'I'm not drinking at the moment.'

'No, I can see that. How do you want it? Pink? Or with water?'

'I've given up drink. That's what I'm saying.'

'Nonsense,' said the Countess, 'you can't have given up drinking.'

'I have, I tell you,' Andrew sprawled in one of the smaller chairs. 'I've given it up altogether. I'm feeling quite ill with the effort of it all.'

'I'm not surprised. But you really shouldn't you know, someone like you, you shouldn't give up gin. You'll get boring, people who've drunk all their lives become terribly, terribly boring once they give it up. In fact "it" gives them up. The thing that makes them tick. You know?'

'No,' said Andrew, but he stopped sprawling for a minute to listen.

'"It" is the thing that makes you get from one place to the other, everyone knows that. Like the petrol in a car.'

'Do you mean the It as in Gin and It, or the It as in – something else?'

'The It as in you, Andrew Gillott, the bit that gets fuelled by the gin, if you give it up you won't go forward, and you'll just become a blubbery mess, won't he Georgiana?'

'Absolutely,' said Georgiana.

'Oh well, in that case, if you're sure it would be bad for me, well, in that case I'll have a pink gin. Thank you.'

'That's a good boy. Georgiana will get it for you, won't you Georgiana, and a nice large gin and tonic for myself, thank you.'

Georgiana poured the drinks as described, omitting any ice, which was anathemetic to both of them, in the same way that gin was to herself. She knew that she would have to get through the pantomime of watching Andrew clowning for the Countess before she would be able to stay on and ask the Countess what had to be asked, or rather tell her what had to be done, and ask for her assistance.

'It's my life,' she told the Countess after Andrew had left to pick up his wife.

'Yes?' said the Countess, and she lit a cigarette, because other people's lives were of great interest to her.

'I'm going to have to do something about it.'

'I'm not surprised.'

Georgiana looked down at her shoes. She was wearing an expensive pair of shoes cut in a slightly twenties style. They gave her great pleasure – the leather was very soft, and the style showed her little ankles to be as perfect as she knew them to be.

'I'm going to have to get married.'

'Nobody nowadays has to get married.'

The Countess looked at her sternly.

'No, that's not what I mean. I mean I'm going to have to get married to someone whom I have not yet met.'

There was a short silence while the Countess sipped her drink carefully, and then put her glass down.

'I see what you mean.'

'I'm going to have to meet someone, soon, or certain things will happen which I don't want to happen.'

The Countess, who disliked Georgiana's mother quite fervently whenever she thought about her, which was infrequently, knew immediately without being told what Georgiana's problem must be. Pressure was coming from a certain quarter, and about time too, although she would not say as much to Georgiana. She sighed a little, deep inside, a small sigh. She knew she would never have a quiet life, and she knew that she did not desire such a thing, but every now and then she felt she might like the luxury of being able to choose whether she wanted it or not.

'Husbands are not as easy to pick up as lovers, you know.'

'Yes, I realise that.'

'Particularly not for you, because you haven't any real money.'

'I realise that too.'

Georgiana's hand touched her gold necklace. It was just as well to be realistic about these things, even if it was humiliating.

'Nevertheless, it shouldn't prove impossible.'

The Countess held out her glass for a second gin.

'You're beautiful, that's always a good start, even if you are a little silly. But then everyone's silly until they're forty, and then they're fearful. However, first things first, and you must get rid of that lover of yours, you'll never attract the right man with him in tow. Next you must start entertaining. I'll do that for you. Give you some background. Don't worry, it'll be fun. Particularly if we're successful.'

She laughed and tapped Georgiana, whom she called 'Georgayna' in the eighteenth-century manner, on the cheek with her hand, although from the way she did it it could have been a furled fan.

Shortly after this Georgiana left her, for she did not want to impose luncheon on her. The Countess watched her leave from her drawing room window. A pretty little thing, it was a great pity that she had not come to her for help before, but then it was first necessary for her to get through her 'kissing taxi drivers' phase, as it used to be known. Now that she was through it, and had savoured the gypsies of this life, she was obviously ready to settle down, and see sense. Or rather sense had been brought to bear upon her, which was hardly before time. She would suffer a little of course, but then everyone did.

'The last time, the very last I tell you, that I find myself going to Peter Jones.'

'Amen to that,' said Andrew, trailing after Clarissa.

She stopped suddenly.

'From now on,' she told the whole of Sloane Square, 'it will be the General Trading Company, or nothing.'

'I favour nothing myself,' murmured Andrew.

They climbed thankfully into a taxi and leant back sighing with relief.

'How was your drink?' asked Clarissa.

'I don't know really. I'd hardly got there when I had to come back and pick you up.'

128

'Even so, how was it?' persisted Clarissa.

'Very nice. A pink gin.'

'No, no. I know what you drink. I mean how was everything *round there*.'

She looked at him significantly.

'Georgiana arrived. Looked a bit fraught.'

'Oh yes? And?'

'And I had to come and pick you up.'

Clarissa tried again.

'I suppose it was something to do with her parents. She has a lot of trouble with those parents, doesn't she?'

'Hang on, they're friends of mine.'

'Even so, she has a lot of trouble with them. I know, Jennifer told me. She spent a fortune of that lover of hers doing the house up, and they still don't like it, apparently. It's strange, isn't it? She and Jennifer, such friends, but since Jennifer became a Marchioness, nothing apparently, absolutely nothing. Not even a telephone call, Jennifer says.'

'Sweet little thing, Georgiana. Very pretty and sweet,' said Andrew, not listening.

'Of course it must be frightfully galling to be the pretty one, and not yet married while Jennifer –'

'Who's as plain as a pike –'

'While Jennifer is so happy with her Pemberton. I mean let's face it, who would have thought it?'

'Georgiana's just more choosy,' said Andrew. 'She didn't pick the first one that popped the question, that's all.'

'Jennifer had other admirers besides Pember, you know that's a fact.'

'They had to be paid to "admire".'

'What do you mean?'

'You know. She had to get fixed up with someone, couldn't attract anyone on her own.'

'She attracted Pemberton all on her own, my dear.'

'Yes, well he was desperate,' said Andrew.

'That's not true.'

'No, but it's not untrue either,' Andrew said, which was a statement so full of philosophical undercurrents that it silenced Clarissa.

Andrew whistled silently through his teeth, and stared out of the window at the newly-cleaned Brompton Oratory as the taxi stop-started its way back to Clarissa's hairdresser. What a life! Trotting after Clarissa all day, carrying her parcels, waiting for her, calling her cabs, but it didn't really mean much nowadays, the boredom didn't really reach him, because he had his 'secret', and Clarissa could say and do what she damn well pleased for it left him as cold as a plate of cold mutton.

'Anyway,' said Clarissa, 'anyway the fact of the matter is that Jennifer is rich, and successful, and married, and Georgiana isn't, and that's the truth of the matter, whichever way you like to look at it.'

Andrew did not like to look at 'it', and so he went on whistling silently to annoy her, which he succeeded in doing admirably. He too had wondered as he left the Countess's house what Georgiana had wanted from her, and he had surmised it must be help of one kind or another, because Georgiana had been very much out of favour with the Countess ever since her fling with that film chap, and so she had to be in some kind of fix to show up at the Countess's house. He just hoped for her sake that it wasn't the kind that had to be given a christening mug.

Georgiana would not have been particularly flattered to know that she was featuring so much in the Gillotts' thoughts. She would not even have been interested. Ever since her affair with Kaminski she had felt little or no interest in what people did or did not have to say about her. Sometimes she wondered whether her disinterest was an extreme form of egoism, or merely a contract that she had made with herself, where in return for not noticing what people said about her, she had promised herself not to listen to what people said about each other.

Obviously if the Countess suspected her of harbouring an unsuitable lover, it would not be long before she would tell someone besides the cat, and that being so she had to free herself from Gus as soon as possible, for he must not discover her deception.

She thought it would be difficult, but she had not calculated for how much his passion for her had moved from the side of his life to the centre.

130

'I don't think we can go on seeing each other,' she began.

'Would you care to repeat that cliché again?'

They had met for a drink, because in her innocence she had thought it would be easier to talk to him somewhere other than his studio. He was right, she was stupid. Heavens knows he had told her enough, one way or another, it was surely time, now that she was leaving him, to tell herself too, and believe it.

'My husband, you know. My husband knows about us, and we can't go on seeing each other.'

She cleared her throat as she finished, and for those few seconds she believed it. She had to, because she knew that he was so much brighter than she was, that unless she believed it, he wouldn't.

'Tell him to get stuffed.'

'It's not as easy as that.'

Gus took her hand. His sincerity was very touching.

'Look, I've been to his stupid house. I've seen how you live. Give it up.'

'I can't. He needs me.'

'Can't you see where the real things in life *really* are?'

'Sssh.'

'I will not "sssh".'

He was shouting now.

'I am not one of your lackeys.'

'You don't understand. You just don't understand.'

'I understand only too well, *Lady Longborough*. You're a greedy little bitch who likes getting her own way. You couldn't give up anything for anyone, not even for yourself.'

'You knew it couldn't be forever.'

'Sure. Oh – go away.'

'Sorry?'

'Go away. Get out. Leave me.'

Georgiana hesitated.

'You've made me feel very cheap.'

'Why? Because I loved you? You shouldn't, that should make you feel good. I'm a great deal more talented and interesting than all those yahoos you're used to.'

'Yes, I know. But –'

'Yes, you know, BUT – but you've got to go back to Lord Yahoo, haven't you? Back to your middle-aged life, and your silly little ways. Well, go back to it – who cares? Not me, least of all me.'

'I'm sorry –'

'Don't be. Your "sorry" is so – nothing.'

Of course neither of them could leave it at that. That had to be the first round, for lovers can seldom make a sharp break, since parting is very much the sweetest of sorrows.

She telephoned him again. Ostensibly it was to say how sorry she was, again, but really it was to hear his voice, which had now, in retrospect, assumed a special quality for her because it was so utterly unlike anything she would be meeting at the Countess's house in succeeding weeks. Naturally he told her to get stuffed.

Then he was sorry.

He was a bastard. He knew it. He just hadn't realised how much he loved her that was all. He couldn't expect her just to leave her husband like that, it was unrealistic. But could he ask her to think about it, he begged? Just to think about it. He loved her, he realised that now. Now that she was no longer around, he ached for her. His pride was terrible. Working-class pride, much worse than anything he had ever accused her of, he said.

Georgiana cried, after he had rung. She cried that she could not love him, that she couldn't be allowed to love him, that she was wicked, that she had deceived him, but as she cried she knew there was nothing that could be done.

But Gus wouldn't leave it at that. He came to her flat, and begged her to leave England with him. They'd go somewhere, somewhere where she could forget that she was married, and he would paint, and it would be wonderful. Even as he spoke he saw that she couldn't believe him, that she would never see life as he did, and this only made him feel a greater love and tenderness towards her, because she was so conventional she couldn't break the rules, not even for love.

To impress her he tried to kill himself, but the painter in the downstairs studio found him, and the hospital gave him a

132

stomach pump. Georgiana was embarrassed. He had gone too far. The doctor said the stomach pump would probably cure him of trying anything so stupid again. It did. It also cured Georgiana.

Chapter Ten

In the country now a light sprinkling of autumn leaves started to feather the front door in front of Patti's house, but there was no buyer for it. She couldn't understand why. She kept it filled with flowers, she showed people round. Sometimes they were enthusiastic and went away declaring their intentions to be honourable, which of course meant that she never heard from them again. Knightey's children rang her every other day, their tones changing from vague deference for her widowhood to open hostility that she had failed to complete a deal. They thought she was common, and often made their thoughts all too apparent.

One day they came and marked the furniture with labels, so that each piece could be identified. They marked the silver too, and then the cutlery, and even those of the curtains that they did not affect to despise. And then finally they each brought a van, and they took the furniture out of the house, piled it into their vans, and left her with a built-in kitchen and a single bed, which she had brought down to the drawing room, so that she could light a fire in the evening and use it as both bed and sofa.

She behaved like a fishwife, they told their friends afterwards, an absolute fishwife. Her language! Talk about blue for Bluebell. Of course, she had everything coming to her. No one had any sympathy for her. No one.

What they didn't know was that she had hidden Knightey's first present to her, good and hidden it too, under the eaves in brown paper, because she didn't trust them not to take everything, which was just as well, since they had, and did. She tried to explain this later to her lawyer, a local fellow, who couldn't help fancying her – not because he wasn't fond of his nice middle-class wife, but because he never saw any crumpet in Stanton, not even on Fridays. Looking at Patti in her leather jodhpurs he started to discover bits of him that his wife didn't even know existed.

'And what was in the parcel, Lady Tisbury?' he asked. 'Something of value?'

Patti nodded, and then very slowly unwrapped the brown paper, several layers of it, until she uncovered an antique cushion. Just for a second this became frightfully exciting, because the lawyer imagined that it must be filled with jewellery.

'His first present to me,' said Patti, and she hugged it to her.

'I see. And it's just – a cushion.'

'The cushion. They took the curtains but they weren't going to take this. They've no right to this, have they?'

'If it's a personal gift of your late husband to you, no, they have no right to it,' agreed the lawyer.

'He was such a generous old sod,' said Patti, tears standing out on the spikes of her mascara.

The lawyer felt a great sense of disappointment as he realised there was no more to the cushion than feathers. He made up for it by imagining Patti without her clothes.

The Pembertons had gone away to Norfolk with Nanny and Charles, and so Patti, in her bare house, tried to meet the challenge of widowhood alone. She joined a local craft guild. Here she found people whom Jennifer had frequently referred to as 'country women'. Patti had never met country women before, and they had never met anyone like Patti before. They treated her in much the same way that they must have treated evacuees during the war. They felt sorry for her, but they knew she would never fit in, and that being so they made every effort to integrate her, in the sure and certain hope that, like the evacuees, she would soon be returning to her native habitat, which was certainly not the country.

Patti did not mind being patronised, because coming from her now bare house and her lonely evenings, days spent labelling jars and counting change were delightful in comparison to lying on her bed torn between watching the little black and white television or listening to the mice running around the eves. On Sundays Fulton and Elliott found time to visit and 'take her out' in true pensioner style.

Patti quickly understood that 'country women' spoke a different language to the rest of the world, and that it was not learnt easily. They left out the subjects that really mattered to other people, such as illness, or widowhood, but they voiced very strong preferences about subjects such as stone-ground bread, juniper berries, herb teas, and different sorts of mustard.

They said 'terribly boring', when she would have said 'tragic', and they made little rude asides about old men and children, which gave everyone to understand that while the rest of the world might sentimentalise about such things, they were not afraid to call a nuisance a nuisance, even if it was too young to understand or too deaf to hear. They attended church, but worshipped at their Agas.

Patti too attended church. She attended church because she felt it brought her nearer to Knightey, and also because it gave her something to do on Sundays before Fulton came to pick her up.

She hadn't been brought up as an Anglican, but she felt since Knightey had this would mean that they would have even more in common when she eventually joined him. She bought a Bible, and searched anxiously through to find a reference to first, or second wives, or both, but she didn't understand most of what was written there, and would so often fall asleep reading it that she privately came to think of it as better than Valium.

She knew the country was far too lonely a place for her to stay as a widow, and that she was too young to be buried there, but there was very little that she could do about it. As the nights became colder the reality of her circumstances became more pressing, because she found she could not work the central heating properly, and she was afraid to ask someone from the village in case they saw her bare boards, and her lack of furniture and fittings. Not even Fulton knew of her circumstances, and she would wait for him at the gate so that he would, hopefully, never know, because she couldn't bear pity along with the cold. Her 'jewellery money' had to be eked out until the lawyers had

136

finished arguing, and she only thanked Knightey in heaven for having been so foolish as to buy her a mink coat, for it was her saving against hypothermia at night.

Her daily help no longer came, and since she had little interest in housework the cobwebs grew, and the dust – a fine light country dust, not unattractive – spread itself over everything. She didn't feel well and she lost weight, because food was not something she wanted. She smoked. And in the evenings before trying to sleep she measured one small scotch into a glass and, sometimes with tears, sometimes with a smile, she toasted herself in the drawing-room mirror, and then retired to bed in her fur.

She had a picture of Knightey which she talked to sometimes. 'How am I doing?' she'd ask him.

Somewhere up above the clouds he answered her, but his replies were so faint, so far away, even her Bible was more understandable.

They'd told her, the estate agents, that there was very little chance of selling the house before spring, now that the furniture was gone. People weren't attracted to empty houses, they said, but once the warmer weather came, and the outside of the house started to look green, and there were roses round the door, or even just daffodils, she would be sure to find a buyer. They treated her with respect, because they thought the money from the house was going to be hers. She didn't tell them that it wouldn't be, and that only one-third of it would be hers, and only then because the children had been allowed to take everything else, and that was how it was all being worked out, because she wanted to keep that respect, and for them to keep thinking that once the house was sold she would be buying another from them, at the same price. It was a kind of lie but that little bit of respect comforted her. She needed it. She knew that it would not be there for long, but while it was, she took it.

There was no way that she could see winter ever ending when her telephone rang one morning, and Jennifer announced that she and Pemberton were back from Norfolk. Patti had not heard from them for some months, and so she acted a little, pretending that she was as much herself as she had ever been, and Jennifer put down the telephone convinced that Patti had very little need of her.

'Funny thing,' she said to Pember, 'but Lady Tizzy is definitely sounding a lot more common now that Sir Gerard's gone. Definitely. Seems to be reverting to type.'

'Really?'

'Yes. Really. It's funny but I believe people do. I read about it in a magazine the other day. Still, I suppose we'll have to ask her up, if I can find a man for her, wouldn't you say?'

Pemberton had very little to say. He had been so bored with Jennifer in Norfolk, he had even taken recourse to bird-watching. A few years before if anyone had ever told him that that was what he would have been doing on a winter afternoon in Norfolk, silently betting on two seagulls making it to a breakwater, he would have told them they were out of their heads. Still, now that it was thankfully over and Jennifer seemed to have had enough of admiring the sea at dusk, the sea at dawn, the sea in storm, and at any other time of day, and he was back at the Hall, he felt things could only look up.

'Yes. Better ask Lady Tizzy up,' said Pemberton. 'Not that she'll have much trouble finding a man again.'

'She will if she's left badly off.'

'Not with her looks, don't you believe it.'

'I've got to go and see my mother today, so I must ask her. Perhaps she'll lend us Andrew, when she's in town next week? That would always do, wouldn't it? Of course we can't ask her up on her own, not just four, we'd better find someone to cover her up with. Another four I think. Heaven knows there are enough people in the County to whom we owe invitations.'

'They're all so boring. Can't you ask someone famous, or different? Not some damn estate agent, or lawyer, or other.'

'Pember, what *do* you mean?'

'What I mean is I get bored with ordinary people – they're so ordinary.'

'Well, they wouldn't *be* ordinary if they were extraordinary, now Pember would they?'

'We never see anyone exciting. If I'm going to see anyone I want them to be exciting.'

'You don't like seeing people. You didn't see any in Norfolk.'

'Exactly. Jolly boring.'

138

Jennifer rose from her place by the telephone. He was annoying her, so she thought she'd go and talk to Nanny. Always the best thing.

Pemberton went into the garden. Always the best thing to do when a woman was getting on your nerves. Not that the garden, at least not the whole garden, not that it gave him as much comfort as it should, for nowadays everywhere he looked he saw the dread hand of Jennifer at work. She would not leave things be. She would neaten and shape, and interfere, so that gradually it was becoming so unrecognisable to him that it made him feel dreadfully upset. He walked nowadays in the piece that had, as yet, not felt the dread hand of his wife.

As he walked he thought about Lady Tizzy, and he thought about the fact that she was a widow, and it gave him other things to think about. Of course it would not be long before she was snapped up again, whatever Jennifer said, and whoever it was that managed to win her would be a very lucky chap. There was a lot to be said for a young body and a kind heart, and he felt that Lady Tizzy had both. Money would be easily acquired when you looked as she did. There would be absolutely no problem in that direction. Anyone with money would want her, and the little matter of her being a bit common could be seen to easily. Although, as a matter of fact, he quite liked that. It made a nice change, something out of the 'ordinary'.

The Gillotts' return to their house was even more fraught than usual because, for once in his life, Andrew had put his foot down. It gave Clarissa a terrible shock. He had never spoken to her rudely before, but when he saw the lampshades she had bought at Peter Jones, he said several offensive things, and then threw them out of the drawing-room window and on to the lawn. What was more, he threatened her. He said if he caught any more of that taste in his house, if you please, he would leave her. Since they had hardly been married a year, Clarissa was appalled. She didn't think of life without Andrew as being anything but utterly bearable, but if he left her at this particular moment, all her friends would laugh at her.

She had become strangely disorientated since she moved from London. Her taste did not seem to please anyone, not even herself. She tried hard to copy everything that Jennifer had at the Hall, but it all kept coming out wrong, and she felt let down by many of the antiques that she had bought, because people kept saying things such as 'Oh dear, the handles have been cleaned.'

Of course she had no ancestors to hang, that went without saying, and there was no doubt about it, they made a great deal of difference. She had thought of having some done at Peter Jones, but since the incident of the lampshades the thought had been banished. As it was, Jennifer kept making little remarks about how funny the faces in the hall looked, because they didn't look like anyone in the house, just as if all the portraits at the Hall were all the spit of her, instead of just being the spit of Pemberton and the baby. Really, it was too much when a person's daughter started to look down on them. Jennifer had no right to make spikey remarks like that, particularly not when she had nothing better to do with her days, it seemed, than to get herself pregnant all the time. Not a very attractive state for a girl to be in permanently.

The life that she had looked forward to living in the country was one of gentility, and acceptability, particularly with a daughter a Marchioness only forty minutes away, but it was all quite different, and not just because of Andrew and the lampshades. To begin with, Wiltshire was much colder than Surrey and London, both of which she had been used to. And then the shops were far away. So far away that spending money had become really quite tedious. And then there was the business of the neighbours. Everyone that lived near the house or in the village was totally horsey. They got up early to take the things out, and then they went to bed at the same time as the wretched things in order that they could get up early to take them out again. Social life seemed to revolve around the horse too. All tickets on sale seemed to be in aid of the Hunt or the Horse. And then when you got to whatever fund raising event it was, all you could see were the same faces that you'd seen the day before trotting by you through the village. That was not what Clarissa called a 'social life'. A social life to her was the serious business of expanding your acquaintanceship to include people to whom you had hitherto, before, not been acceptable.

At all events Andrew was not any help, for neither did he ride, nor did he shoot, and racing which he did do was about as interesting to Clarissa as macramé was to him.

Some things she had managed by copying from a catalogue. For instance the morning room, she had copied that from a catalogue, the Laura Ashley catalogue, and it had seemed to come out right, even though Andrew refused to sit in it because he said it made him feel as if he'd had a sex change. Nevertheless, Clarissa felt it was right when she sat in it to do her macramé, and lately she had made a practice of sitting in it to receive Jennifer, because it was currently the only room that Jennifer did not level some unspoken criticism at.

Nowadays she had a way of swivelling her eyes as she sat down which made Clarissa most uneasy.

'Is that new?'

She picked up a little object that Clarissa had trouvé in an antique shop in Stanton.

'No, it's quite old, I believe. William IV they said.'

'William IV!'

Jennifer laughed lightly. A little minute went by. Clarissa was determined not to say anything, not a word.

'Everything is William IV.'

Jennifer laughed again. Clarissa really couldn't see what was so terribly funny.

'The poor old chap reigned for all of something like three years, and so rather than say "Victorian", they always say "William IV".'

This was not Jennifer, and Clarissa knew it. This was Pemberton speaking, but what could she do? She couldn't disprove it. She couldn't say, 'You don't know what you're talking about,' because, since it was Pemberton she was obviously quoting, and he did, it meant that Jennifer, even if she didn't, did, because of him. Clarissa pushed her needle into her canvas, and caught her finger. The pain was considerably less than that which Jennifer was causing.

'You're going to London next week, aren't you?'

Clarissa nodded without speaking.

'Good, then you could bring me back a little suit I saw for Charles in Beauchamp Place, couldn't you?'

'I think I might be a bit busy for that.'

'Really? In that case I'll ask Nanny to go up and get it for me. Don't worry.'

Andrew came in. Jennifer smiled at him.

'Hallo, step-father,' she said.

Andrew, not expecting her, smiled suddenly. Not that he particularly liked Jennifer, but it was such a change to see someone besides her wretched mother.

'She been telling tales on me?'

'How do you mean?'

'Hasn't she told you about my chucking all her lampshades on the compost?' asked Andrew proudly.

'No! You naughty fellow!'

Andrew nodded.

'Yes, chucked the lot on the compost.'

'Never mind, get some more soon,' said Jennifer in her 'baby voice'. 'Tell you what though. I hear you're being left to fend for yourself next Tuesday. Mrs Gillott's going to London for the night, yes?'

'Don't ask me,' said Andrew, 'I haven't the slightest idea.'

'Yes, well apparently that's how it is, so what about popping across to have dinner with us?'

'Who will look after the cat?' asked Clarissa.

'Bugger the cat,' said Andrew, 'course I'll come. Great fun.'

'Good. Poor Lady Tizzy's going to be there, and she does so need cheering up.'

'I don't think it's Tuesday I'm going to London after all, as a matter of fact –'

'Yes, it is,' said Andrew, 'it's Tuesday all right. I know, because you've got the dentist all that day, and you said you'd go and lie down at the flat afterwards.'

'So it's "yes" then?'

'Rather.'

'Good.'

Jennifer smiled. Andrew nodded. Clarissa's needle pierced her finger for the second time.

'So now we'll put the boring Major Williams next to Lady Tizzy,' murmured Jennifer to herself a week later. 'And then we'll put Mrs Williams next to Andrew, and Andrew next to Elizabeth –'

She stopped because Bloss had come into the room, and she never liked him to overhear anything of inconsequence.

'The table's very nice, Bloss,' she said, 'but —'

She looked sideways at him. Sometimes she wasn't quite certain of what Bloss was thinking, which could be aggravating in the same way that she felt that he didn't like her, but she couldn't be sure, if only she could be sure, then she could ask Pemberton to dismiss him, but since she wasn't, she couldn't.

'*But*, mi-lady?'

'But, yes, but I see one of the chairs is, are, broken.'

Bloss trod round to the point where the erring chair stood. He picked it up. Then he put it down.

'It's only a little broken, mi'lady.'

'Oh well,' said Jennifer hurriedly, 'if it's only a little broken, then it can't be helped.'

Bloss stood back. Jennifer peered at one of the names in front of her side of the table, and promptly picked it up, and took it round to his side, and placed it in front of the broken chair.

'Yes, well that should be all right, now, I think,' she said, and she went out of the room.

Bloss looked at the name in front of him. It was his turn to pick it up. Now he took it back to where it had been originally. He wasn't having any of that.

Patti's feelings towards going to dinner with the Pembertons were mixed. Pleased that she was going out, but sorry that it had to be the Pembertons in whose house lay so many memories of a very bored Knightey. Now that the Big G. was no longer with her she had no idea of how to dress for a formal evening, and she was too afraid of making a fool of herself to ring and ask, suspecting that might invite condescension, and also the wrong information, which was not unheard-of on such occasions. 'Just a wool frock', and when you turned up they were all in their tiaras. Last week she had worn her leather mini skirt to the cake stall and invited a paean of condescending remarks.

With Knightey everything had been different, for he had a most eccentric line in old wool knickerbockers, and strange baggy trousers, and yet the way he wore them forbade any criticism.

'Dress to please me,' Knightey would yell into her cupboard, 'you can never go far wrong if you do.'

But he was no longer there to be pleased, and so she laid out her most expensive dress, and hoped that it would be in good taste, whatever that was, for although the label could not be worn on the outside, nevertheless it was quite obviously well-cut and expensive.

She no longer had any of her little diamonds and things that Knightey had given her, just her gold wedding band, but it didn't really matter, because now that Knightey was gone there was no one to pin them on her, or do up the catches while she lifted her hair. Getting dressed had become quite different.

In the bath she rehearsed conversations that she might have.

'Have you read Muriel Knight's recent book? No? Oh it's very good, quite as good as her last, I thought.'

'I see that the Sheikh has had twenty winners over hurdles already, isn't that amazing?'

It was just stuff she had seen in the newspaper, but it was a start, because Knightey had taught that she had to start somewhere, and therefore where didn't matter, just so long as people were given the opportunity to say 'yes' or 'no', or whatever, and there was no suggestion to anyone that you were what the ladies at the craft guild called a 'bore'. Except they said it '*boar*'.

'Such a *boar*,' they said, about everything, except Agas.

Knightey's children had left her the Mini. They had to because she could prove she'd paid for it, otherwise she'd have been walking up to the Hall. She stopped and bought some cigarettes, and then she drove slowly up to the great doors, her heart beating faster than normal, half in dread, half in excitement, because she had not been out at night since the silly sod had died, God bless him.

'Good evening, Lady Tisbury.'

She'd got the butler's number all right.

'Evening Bloss. How's tricks?'

Bloss smiled.

'Tricks is fine your ladyship, it's life's that's the pain.'

'Careful with the stink,' Patti called after him. 'I'm not likely to get another of them, you know.'

'Fret not, mi'lady, I shan't feed it to pussy.'

'Am I the last?'

'Yes, but County before quality, I always say.'

Patti looked at him.

'Here, will I do?'

'If mi'lady was a fillet she'd be à point.'

He opened the drawing-room door, and then watched her sidle into the room. Poor bitch, as if it wasn't bad enough the old man dying on her like that, to die and leave her penniless, that was a beastly bit of luck, even if she did deserve it.

Conversation had reached the second gin and tonic stage. It was animated and aimless. Jennifer was well-pleased. Everything was just as it should be, although nothing was better than Patti, who couldn't have looked more inappropriate. The trouble with people like Patti was that they never 'got it right'. They always managed to stand out in quite the wrong way. Pember couldn't take his eyes off her, quite obviously because she was completely out of place. The only time Patti had managed to look tasteful was at her poor husband's funeral, when she had managed to look suitable, quite by mistake.

And so into dinner, once Patti had gulped, there was no other word for it, her sherry. Jennifer's place names were all in order, the flowers and the candles perfectly arranged, because she had checked everything just before the first arrival, but now it became clear to her that they had all been changed, and by some unseen hand, for Patti had been placed beside Pemberton.

'Oh dear Pember,' said Jennifer a little too loudly, 'I'm afraid there's been a mistake.'

'What's that?'

'There's been a mistake. The "placement" has gone all wrong. I distinctly remembered putting Lady Tizzy over there —'

Jennifer pointed across the room.

'And now Elizabeth is where Lady Tizzy should be.'

'Does it matter?'

'Well, yes, as a matter of fact, I wanted Patti to have the broken chair.' She smiled.

'Elizabeth has a bad back,' she explained generally, 'so we can't do that to her can we?'

'Oh pooh,' said Pemberton, 'let's all sit, for heaven's sake.'

'No Pember,' said Jennifer firmly, 'I'm afraid not.'

'I don't mind,' said Patti, 'I like broken chairs.'

There was a silence.

'Twenty past or twenty to?' asked Jennifer, and they all sat down.

Patti put her cigarettes on the table in front of her.

'You don't mind if I have an "intercourse"?' she asked her neighbour. 'I'm afraid I'm smoking for England since my husband died.'

'I'm afraid I do,' said Jennifer, and she patted her front, indicating her pregnancy.

Patti quickly put her cigarettes back into a handbag bulging with old letters.

'Sure, do me good to wait till I get home,' she said.

Jennifer smiled slightly. What a good thing she had decided to 'cover' the poor girl up. A foursome with just herself and Pember and Andrew would have been a disaster, absolute disaster. As it was, it was not going to be the smoothest of evenings, for heavens knows what they would all find to say to Patti when the ladies retired, but no doubt they would. Later, much later, she would make every effort to find out whom had rearranged the placement cards, and if it was 'whom' she suspected, there would be dreadful repercussions.

Andrew had never enjoyed himself more. Life had taken on a lovely pink-gin colour from the moment Lady Tizzy had hoved into view, and since he had had the good luck to sit on her left during dinner, it had stayed his favourite colour, right up until the moment when the memsahibs had retired. The other women were an ugly lot of stuffy creatures, the sort that had lost the Empire for Britain because they didn't know how to treat the natives, but that was only to be expected since Jennifer was very much that type herself. Lady Tizzy was something else.

After dinner the gentlemen joined the ladies in double-quick time. Jennifer was furious with Pember. It was so typical of him. She had hardly had time to introduce topics like raspberry vinegar and Agas, topics that she knew would be well outside Patti's range, and use words like 'on the hoof', good country women's words, when the men burst through the doors all set to

146

join the ladies. It was terribly, terribly irritating, particularly since when Pember was on his own he stayed in the dining room for hours.

Perhaps it was as a consequence of this that coffee and brandy proved a deadly dull part of the evening, so that everyone was encouraged to look at their watches, and discover that it was well past the time that they should have been home. Jennifer, who hated anything except the earliest nights, was actually immensely relieved to see them all go. She had really only asked them to help out with Patti, and now that that was done, she could stand in the hall watching the guests departing and the rain falling down, with the kind of calm that can only come to a person who has done their duty, and won't have to do it again for a very long time.

The door closed finally. Minutes later Bloss opened it again.

'My Mini won't start,' said Patti. 'It hates the wet, the stupid thing.'

Pemberton jumped into action.

'No problem,' he called, 'I'll take you, I'll take you.'

And before Jennifer had time to suggest that Bloss could drive her home, he was out of the front door, and guiding her towards the stables where he kept his Porsche.

As soon as they were alone together in the Porsche Pemberton's lovely warm feeling returned. Patti was still so sensational. She smelt beautiful too, of scent that reminded him of no one but herself. Her dress had been the sensation of the evening, and now here they were alone together. Pemberton, Patti and the Porsche. All during 'Norfolk' he had half-expected that she would change, and that when they returned to the Hall, when Jennifer at last allowed them to return to the Hall, he would find that he had built up this glorious creature, and that she didn't really exist, but no, she was still as shapely, still as much the embodiment of everything that a man fantasised over, well out of sight of his marriage.

As he changed gears he gazed at her. As she spoke to him he widened his eyes in the darkness. He knew that he was good-looking, that he held attractions for the opposite sex, and that there were certain ways that he could show them that he would not be averse to their returning the attractions he felt for them.

'Would you mind if I had a cigarette?' she asked.

Even her smoking, somehow so unattractive in other women, was not unattractive in her.

'Of course not,' he said, while mentally noting to tell them to air the Porsche the following morning.

'That was quite some evening,' she said through her smoke.

'Yes, I enjoyed it,' he said.

'Want to come in for a drink?'

'Yes, I would enjoy that.'

'Scotch is about all I can offer you, I'm afraid,' she said, 'and you'll need it by the time you've been in Flint House for more than a minute.'

He didn't know what she meant, until he saw what she meant. 'They took everything.'

He looked round the drawing room. Bare boards, bare windows, just a little bed with a cover in front of the fire.

'It saves dusting.'

Patti smiled.

'Don't tell anyone, though will you? I mean I don't mind you knowing because you're so rich, you'll understand, but the others –'

'You poor little thing,' said Pemberton, and that lovely warm feeling went and, possibly because the room was cold, it was replaced by something stronger and more passionate.

'You poor little thing,' he said again.

Jennifer took her earrings from her rather too small ear lobes, and placed them delicately in the old leather case with faded monogram, which housed her sensational but not extensive collection of jewels. Pember would be back any minute, and when he was they would have some fun discussing the evening, but until that moment she would lie in bed and happily remember Patti and her discomfiture; the way she quite obviously felt out of her depth, the way she looked so *out of place*. It was most amusing.

She fell asleep long before she meant to. She was asleep when Pember returned, and in the morning she was too busy getting to the bottom of the business of the 'placement' cards to discuss Patti with Pember, or to find out at what time he had returned.

Chapter Eleven

Weekends in the country had changed since Georgiana had placed herself back in the market place. They were no longer spent in almost secrecy at Longborough, attempting to enjoy herself away from the glare of her parents' view, but once more in other people's houses. It was necessary. She was never going to meet anyone suitable in her own house, of that she could be quite sure.

She had always had considerable charm, and now it was that she remembered it. She made up to her weekend hostesses for her charm and her beauty, by the lavish quality of her house presents. She brought them too much of everything, so that whenever they saw the box of Bendick's chocolates long after she had gone, they would remember and smile, because it was by far the biggest that they had been given lately. They couldn't accuse her of vulgarity, as they might someone else, just generosity, of the kind that was, in their minds, thoroughly aristocratic, which so many of them weren't.

Sometimes Georgiana became depressed. It wasn't just being back in the market place looking for a suitable husband, having to pretend that she wasn't, particularly because she was, but because there seemed to be no one even proper around any more. There were plenty of brokers, plenty of 'Johnny-cum-riches' as the Countess referred to them, but no one 'proper'. No one like Charles II with whom she had had an imaginary but passionate affair at the age of fourteen.

Her availability and the renewed threat to Longborough necessarily sent her to see Mary.

Outside her house the bay trees still grew, a little sprinkling of road dust ornamenting their leaves which were only ever polished for parties. Inside the drawing room had changed, some of the paintings were unmistakably masculine choices, and there was a greater strictness in the artless arrangements of the 'objets'.

'Men always succeed in making rooms look like dentists' waiting rooms,' the Countess often remarked.

The men in Mary's life, if rumour was true, had not succeeded in making her drawing room reminiscent of high-speed drills, but nevertheless there was something that had happened, something that was struggling to assert itself, that was not of Mary's choosing. The flowers were still white, and the books were carefully chosen for their acceptable covers and newness of publication, but now there was a carefully embroidered cushion with a rude message on it which would not be 'Mary', and a copy of the Racing Calendar in the wastepaper basket, also not 'Mary'.

Georgiana mocked her younger self as she remembered how only a brief two years before she had been so impressed by Mary's taste. It had seemed so sophisticated, so unattainable, not as it seemed now, a little predictable, a little careful, nearly ready to set, not unlike Mary, who was now fetching a small drink while Lucius found her a small conversation.

'I gather you're having problems?'

Lucius said 'problems' in a particularly American way that made him sound as if he was a medical consultant, not a failed novelist.

'Not really,' said Georgiana. 'My life's in need of direction, that's all.'

She thought it impertinent of Lucius to talk about her 'problems' openly as if he was some kind of agony auntie, and she a young girl writing in to him. She also resented the fact that Mary had obviously found out her predicament from the Countess, and had talked about it to Lucius, who was not a member of her family. She smiled at Lucius, because she really rather hated him.

The lighting grew brighter as Hugo came in. He was too handsome, Georgiana decided, as she kissed the air beside him.

There was a point when a man really could be too handsome, when his looks became affected and unbelievable, as a person whose manners are too good. Even so he was always immediate fun. He never waited, but scintillated from the minute he made his entrance to the moment he exited.

'What is your worst nightmare?' he asked Georgiana. 'The unspoken terror that comes to you in the night. Nothing silly allowed now, like the world blowing up. It must be personal.'

'Not realising that I have something on my teeth at a dinner party.'

'Good, very good. Lucius?'

Lucius thought for a moment.

'I'm at a very grand occasion, and I open my mouth to say something, and I'm sick.'

'Yes, that's good. Mary?'

'You know mine –'

'Yes, of course, the thing that happened to your great-aunt, she popped to the loo, then went to make a great entrance without realising that her dress was caught up at the back –'

'Ghastly.'

Mary shuddered.

'Luckily someone saw in time,' she told Georgiana.

'Come on, Hugo, what about you?'

'That's easy, waking up and finding I can't stand my own smell!'

'But you don't smell.'

'I thought my nose smelt of cheese the other day. I nearly topped myself.'

Mary stood up. She sensed she must terminate the conversation there, for Hugo had the habit of going too far, too early, and she did not think it suitable to let him in front of Georgiana.

'Shall we go into lunch?'

She swung her dark hair back as she walked in front of Georgiana, and Georgiana thought that she really ought to cut it a little because it was becoming just a little 'déjà vu'.

They climbed down the spiral staircase to the dining room, and the familiar smell of Mary's luncheons came back to Georgiana. Salads, soufflés, a hint of something foreign in the oil. The luncheon preparations had often, in the past, been Georgiana's task, and she would stand at the dining hatch between courses trying to catch something of the conversations, and wondering when, as a poor cousin, she would at last be allowed to sit at the table, rather than stand in the kitchen? Through her eavesdropping she would hear financial tips but be unable to follow them, listen to talk of 'abroad' knowing she could not afford it, and try to follow gossip about people she had never met. It had all seemed pretty hopeless, until Kaminski had come into her life. Now it was not so very much better, but at least she was at the table, at least she was out from behind the serving hatch. She had made a little progress creeping up behind Grandmother Fortune's back, a little nearer, but still not quite able to touch her on the shoulder.

After lunch they drew up a list of suitable men for Georgiana. It was hilarious, to them. No one thought of consulting her for preferences, but turned themselves to the problem with all the concentration that comes naturally to those who are idle. Men appeared on the list who had money, who had property, who had both, but none appeared on the list who were not discovered to have a flaw.

'It's rather frighteningly short,' said Mary.

'I don't think we're trying hard enough,' said Hugo.

'No, no, that's not fair, we have tried, we've tried very hard, but there are so few normal men around,' said Lucius.

At which point everyone laughed.

'There's no one here that *I'd* want, but how desperate are you?' asked Hugo.

'I'm not desperate,' said Georgiana, 'but I'm looking.'

'Who isn't?' asked Hugo. 'What about me then? I'm handsome, a little rich and I'd never make demands.'

'You're not rich enough,' said Mary quickly. 'Have you seen Longborough?'

Hugo sighed.

'Perhaps you're right,' he agreed.

Georgiana decided to leave. Mary was not quite pleased. She never liked people to make their own decisions, and she never liked people to leave until she indicated that they could.

'Oh very well,' she said in a clipped kind of way.

Georgiana let herself out into the street, shutting the front door quietly after her, and as she did so she imagined the laughter that would still be surrounding some of the names on the list. She was terribly unhappy. There were very few normal men. That is men who were sexually normal, or not too old or on a drug cure. Men who would want to get married to her for the right reasons, and not for the wrong, for the men who would want to marry her for the wrong reasons would not be suitable.

The Countess too had made a list, which she presented to Andrew in exchange for some old windfalls that Clarissa had sent up from the country as proof that she had an orchard.

'They've all got holes in them,' said the Countess peering into the basket.

'So have most of these,' said Andrew staring at her list. 'What the devil does Georgiana want to get married for anyway, doesn't she know it's the end of everything?'

'It's her "ancestors", they're putting pressure on,' said the Countess, throwing the apples on the fire.

'Her mother and father are a couple of old stuffed shirts,' said Andrew. 'They hunt too much. Hunting people leave their brains in their caps. Give me racing people any day, but hunting people who don't race, they give me the pip.'

'Her parents haven't been on a horse for years, you old fool. No, that's not their problem, their problem is they're sour. People who are sour like to sit down and think up grievances, and tell sad tales of the death of kings.'

'Well, there's no problem, not with Georgiana, should find someone, shouldn't she?'

'Yes, but we don't want her to find just someone, we want her to find some*body*. She's my niece, you know.'

'Thought you didn't have much time for her?'

'I don't, she's a silly creature at the best of times, but she's my niece.'

Andrew picked up the list.

'Shall we start at the top then? Oh no, he won't do – he may be a Duke, but he's round the twist.'

'I thought you'd said he'd had that treatment, that they'd put those things on his head?'

'They did, but it didn't work. Next – good God, old Billy – you know he's over eighty of course? And David Shepton, he's on his third already, and can't remember anyone, not even his wives, because he's always footless.'

Andrew put down the Countess's list.

'Tut, tut, you're losing your touch, mi'lady, this list ain't worth the ink you've wasted on it.'

The Countess looked at the bottom of her glass, and then she got up and helped them both to another gin.

'You're right, my heart's not been in it lately. Find I keep getting time lapses, you know, back a generation. Still, mustn't give up.'

A second gin cosily ensconced in their glasses, they began again, sitting with their address books, and the up-to-date volume of *Debrett*, for all the world like two old age pensioners, as the Countess remarked, with their football coupons. It was quite like the old days, and as they murmured their way through the old names, and some of the newer ones, they both remembered how much fun they had had together in previous seasons. Pushy debutante mothers besieging them for suitable escorts for their daughters, the dreadfully ugly daughters of politicians trying to find themselves husbands, catering services badgering them to make them fashionable, sums offered for introductions, the City ever eager to 'up' themselves in each other's eyes.

'I don't know why we ever stopped,' said Andrew.

'Had enough suddenly, you remember? And you went off to wherever it was, and I didn't have the energy to go on.'

'No, you didn't, did you? Course we always under-charged, didn't we?'

'We had fun.'

'Once Clarissa's off my hands we'll get back –'

'How about dumping her on a sheikh?'

'What as, a camel?'

'That won't be long now, will it?'

'It'll take one generation at Eton.'

'Of course. Drink up. Mustn't be too late for the R.A., you know, you get run down by eager ladies in sandals from Rye.'

At the Royal Academy preview Andrew sighed as he

followed the Countess into the first room.

'I'm having a drink when I get to number fifty, because I always do,' he said.

'I know everything about Art,' said the Countess, 'but I don't know what I like.'

'That's horrible,' said Andrew, and walked off to find a drink even though they were only at number twenty-eight.

He was on about his third when he looked up and saw someone he knew staring at him. He walked away and then came back. Yes, there was no doubt about it, it was Georgiana, and she was staring at him from a picture, from two pictures, and she hadn't got a stitch on, not in either of them. He quickly went and sat down in another room. What on earth had happened to Georgiana? Was she so desperate that she had to parade herself in this way? It made her look so cheap, an artist's moll of the most dreadful kind. He couldn't get to grips with the thing. It was worse than being on a calendar. He hurried off to find the Countess who was in the miniature room noting down someone's name.

'What's that?'

'What's that?' said Andrew. 'That's Georgiana, I tell you, without a penny piece of clothing.'

The Countess stared at 'Odalisque I' and 'Odalisque II'. The silly old fool was right, it was Georgiana. She turned to Andrew, who was rattling the change in his pocket and puffing a little.

'At least they're both sold,' she said.

'Is that all you can say?' said Andrew walking after her and elbowing everyone out of his way. 'There's your niece cavorting around the Royal Academy without a stitch, and that's all you can say?'

'I think you're being very middle class,' said the Countess. 'It's not as if she hasn't got a good body.'

'But everyone can see what she looks like –'

'And very nice too.'

'But don't you see. It means she's – it means that chap, whoever he was, he painted her without, you can't say it's normal. It's not. Don't care what you say.'

'What I say is –' said the Countess, 'it's always gone on.'

'There'll be a dreadful scandal,' said Andrew putting his

umbrella up with a snap, 'and now we'll never get a cab.'

'Not nowadays there won't,' said the Countess. 'And anyway, who's to say who the girl in the picture *is*. They don't give her name, do they?'

'No, that's true.'

'Now let's have lunch and talk about something else.'

'I don't know,' said Andrew, 'it's all a bit "Lady Hamilton" for me, and look what happened to her.'

'Whatever we do,' she declared, 'we must remember to make a note of who, or whom, put his little red stickers all over those paintings.'

'What do you mean?'

'What I mean,' said the Countess walking on now, 'is that he might, just might, be someone as suitable as anyone else on our lists.'

Naturally she was not unhappy to discover that he was rich, and a baron, he had inherited a small fortune from a relation of his mother's, and consequently lived in London, Scotland, and Kent, which although not ideal, would be forgiven, if you also lived in Scotland, and London. His name was James Stranragh. She sent him an invitation to her cocktails. Or, as Andrew rudely referred to it, her 'charity party' in aid of Georgiana.

Gus had sent 'Odalisque I and II' to the R.A. because he despised it, and he hoped that the paintings, which he also now despised, would shock the society poodles and yahoos, and particularly the sitter's husband. What he hadn't anticipated was that they should sell on the first day, and that the purchaser would invite him to dinner.

As he dressed to meet him, choosing his clothes with unusual care, he wondered what sort of man he would be? A lover of women's bodies obviously, or he wouldn't have bought two paintings of the same figure. A person who bought modern paintings, which coming from his background was slightly unusual, since most of them only bought from the meat men after you were dead.

He walked to the man's house. Lately it had become a habit with him. He had been reading books on mysticism and on zen buddhism. As he walked, he was the pavement, he was the sky above, he was the bus that he passed, he was a tree, he was the bell that he pushed.

The house was white, informal in its chic, and worth a fortune. Stranragh opened the door himself. The hall was larger than the outside of the house proclaimed. It was also dark, made darker by a collection of icons, always a strange taste, Gus thought. The furniture sat upon a fashionable form of sisal, and the room in which they had their drinks was more library than drawing room.

Gus would have liked to have hated his host but he was not a man who was despised easily. He had been a racing driver until he had had a bad accident, which he called 'accident' rather than 'smash'. Neither was he a 'civilian' in the artistic sense. His collection of paintings reflected a person of judgement, and also a man who was prepared to take a risk. They discussed the loss of European Art to the American Collectors. It was quite a dull conversation.

Perhaps because polite conversation irritated him, Gus began to wonder where the paintings, his paintings, were? Not that he liked them particularly, but nevertheless he liked to see them. Not that he would ask. Not that he would admit to wanting to ask. He was so bored by rich people. They bored him to his marrow. They were like wall-to-wall carpeting. They deadened sound, they deadened reality. They had special conversations for every occasion. They knew nothing about anything outside their own desires. They weren't moved by anything, except poverty, from which they moved away.

'Shall we go in?'

Gus followed Stranragh into the dining room where a large woman smelling faintly of onions was laying the inevitable avocado pears with prawns. He would have preferred Gravlax. His dealer always served Gravlax. He associated Gravlax with going to expensive addresses.

'Odalisque I' was hung over the large Edwardian sideboard. It had a little light of its own, which shone upon Georgiana's buttocks, and upon her breasts, rounded, but with nipples of not too large a size, and it reminded Gus of summer, and of peaches; and the loveless dining room, the pale musty look of the avocados, and the rather too small prawns in their rather too pink sauce made him feel nauseous. Christ, how he had loved her!

Georgiana didn't suit the place. He wanted to take the painting from the wall, and throw it outside into the street, out of this lifeless room. She should be somewhere where she could breathe air. He pushed his food away. His manners were not of the same kind as his host's, and he failed to see why he should attempt to even pretend that they were. The room was too hot, and the wine was too heavy, and although Stranragh was obviously civilised – perhaps because Stranragh was so obviously civilised – they had nothing in common.

He was talking.

'I said, when would you be free?'

He wanted Gus to paint a fresco in his house in Italy. Jesus, how many houses did he have?

'Now. Tomorrow?'

'It would mean going away for more than a few weeks. Being out of England for a fairly long time.'

'So?'

Gus shrugged his shoulders, and pushed his chair away from the table.

'If you come with me, I'll show you some photographs.'

Gus left the dining room with a feeling that he needed to walk somewhere where there was air. Talk about claustrophobia. Zen buddhism was no help either. Who the hell wanted to be an avocado pear, or a prawn?

The house in Italy was an elegant little villa. Stranragh wanted the centre room, or 'atrium' as he called it, from which all other rooms led, painted with the fresco. He made no suggestions as to what Gus should paint, for which Gus had to be grateful. He did however set a time limit.

'Of course you will be able to do some of your own work, and there's a cottage in the grounds.'

'There always is.'

Stranragh smiled briefly. Painters. They were all the same 'Cave Canem.' Not that Mr Hackett was dislikeable. He suffered from what the French called 'âme de colere', but he did not seem untrustworthy. Neither did he drink or eat to excess.

Neither did he talk about himself. A disciplined man hanging on to his anger with white knuckles. It amused Stranragh to watch him.

They made arrangements with suspicious ease. Gus would be paid in England. His fee was not outrageous. Neither was it cheap. He would live rent free, and his food and drink would be taken care of, as would also his expenses for driving out to Tuscany, and his materials. The deal would be formalised in writing, and he could leave as early as he wished since there was a housekeeper who came in every day, who would take care of him on arrival.

'I don't think there's anything else,' said Stranragh eventually. 'Would you like a cognac?'

'Yes, I would.'

He felt safe to drink now. Italy, Tuscany, everything that a change could bring, calmed him. Life could turn corners. It didn't always make a corner out of you. In Italy he would drink grappa, he would watch fireflies, he would paint dark skins, oil-thickened black hair, he would grow long fingernails and dwell upon the *Ode to a Nightingale*.

He murmured in his head:

'O for a beaker of the warm South,
Full of the true, the blushful Hippocrene –'

'Did you know,' he said suddenly to his host, 'did you know that the *Ode to a Nightingale* is actually better in Italian?'

'It would be difficult to believe.'

'Do you speak Italian?'

'No.'

'That is a pity, for if you did I could prove it to you.'

Gus stood up. He had had enough. He would not thank Stranragh. He would wait for the deal in writing, and then he would thank him. They shook hands. As he left Gus felt safe enough to glance through the dining room door to where Georgiana lay upon the wall. It was a deliberate gesture of farewell. Stranragh watched him.

'Would it be indiscreet to ask for the name of the lady?'

'Lady Georgiana Longborough.'

'I've been away a great deal, I can't say I've met her.'

'Don't.'

'Am I to understand that you knew her slightly better than most?'

'You are.'

'She's very beautiful.'

'She's a whore.'

'You had an affair?'

'Only during the week, don't you know? At weekends her ladyship went home to hubby.'

'Did he know?'

'I don't know. Yes. He must have. I don't know. Who cares? Who fucking cares?'

He tried to open Stranragh's door, and failed. It was a mass of locks. Stranragh opened it for him. Gus fell into the street. He was the sky, he was the stars, and soon he would be Italy. He began the long walk back to his studio.

Stranragh looked up 'LONGBOROUGH, Georgiana Rose' in one of his reference books, and then he went and stood in front of 'Odalisque II'.

This painting he kept to himself. It hung in his bedroom opposite his steel-framed bed, upon his brown suede walls. It was more sensuous than the first painting, the painting that hung in the dining room. In this one it was obvious that she had just been made love to. 'She.' He had always called her 'she', but now he could call her 'Georgiana'. And she was not married.

Chapter Twelve

'I'm going to have to sit down. I am going to have to sit.'

Elliott sat down.

'For heaven's sake, anyone would think you were the father.'

Fulton stood looking out of the window on to the view of the square. A view he had become really tired of. It had too little green. Some green, but not enough. And Bath was getting a tiny bit old for him, now that he was a tiny bit older. And at night it was so dull and flat that you had to get on a train, and go to London, and *do* something, rather than just sit around waiting for the telephone not to ring. Doing nothing was a nothing occupation. Which was not what he proposed to do about Patti, poor child. He could not sit around and do nothing about her. No money, no furniture, a car, although hardly what you'd *call* a car, and now this frightful news of her pregnancy. What would happen to her? Who would look after her? She was talking about going back to London, which on the face of it was very sensible, except for the fact that with the money that she had to spend she would be able to buy one room overlooking the Isle of Dogs. Hardly a good beginning for her tiny bump.

'But how did it happen?' asked Elliott.

'I should imagine in exactly the same way, more or less, that these things usually happen,' said Fulton icily, 'And no, I don't know whom the father is, nor do I care.'

'The poor child, the poor child,' said Elliott.

'Elliott,' said Fulton, 'grim though this news may be, I must ask you not to carry on as though you were a maiden aunt who had just been told her niece was giving birth to a baby on the wrong side of the blanket.'

'But I feel so sorry for her.'

'That is fairly evident.'

'What will she do?'

'Knowing Patti, everything that she shouldn't. She is completely unfit to bring up a child. She is completely unfit to bring herself up. And far too soft to contemplate anything except having it. No question of gin in the bath.'

'So what will she do? What shall *we* do?'

'We'll help her the best way that we can, that's what we'll do.'

'And how can we do that?'

'Do you know, Elliott, I really rather hate this view.'

'So do I,' said Elliott quickly.

'I think we should sell this flat, and go and live in the country.'

'But Bath *is* the country.'

'I mean with moo-cows, and things.'

'What about the shop?'

'Keep the shop. Commute. Well?'

Elliott stood up. He pressed his hands together.

'I know what you're going to say – I know – you're going to say we're going to buy Flint House, aren't you?'

'What a clever person. Spot on.'

'Oh all right, we'll buy Flint House, but that only helps Patti so far, but no further. I mean, what about where she's going to live? You can't fork out more than market price, and that still only leaves her with her tiny little purse, and her tiny little baby.'

There was a long silence, during which Fulton tried to pretend that the solution to everything wasn't already upon his lips waiting to pop out, and that Elliott didn't know it, and that he didn't know that Elliott knew it.

'One of us is going to have to marry her.'

Fulton looked across from the window at Elliott.

'It's the only solution.'

'You're right. It is.'

'Good. Now the only question is which one of us will become official "father"?'

'You're the oldest.'

'And therefore the most wise –'

'On insurance grounds it should really be me –' said Elliott.

'You're too flighty to be a father.'

'Suppose we ask Patti?'

'Absolutely not. We have to decide between ourselves and then *tell* Patti. If you ask Patti anything she'll answer yes, no, and maybe, and you'll be back to square one. Besides, she's in no mood to make up her own mind, her mind must be made up for her. And that's that.'

'Yes, you're right,' agreed Elliott. And then reluctantly he said, 'I think she might prefer you.'

Fulton smiled at Elliott.

'That's very sweet of you, but no, we must be fairer than that. Let's toss. Heads you're going to be hubby, and tails I'm going to be hubby. How about that?'

'Yes.'

'You've gone a paler shade of grey!'

'So have you. How about a drink?'

'De rigeur, my dear.'

'Good. Cocktails and laughter, spin the coin, then drive and tell Patti the good news.'

'We'll have to be prepared, whatever the outcome, that she might be shaken, not stirred?'

'Quite prepared. But nonetheless, when she's stopped crying, she'll be terribly pleased and grateful, don't you think?'

'As long as we don't tell her we tossed for her!'

'Yes. *Not* a good idea.'

'Oh dear, when this gets out what a brou-ha-ha!'

They started to laugh.

Fulton won the toss.

Patti greeted the news that Fulton was going to marry her with the same lack of calm that she had greeted the news that she was pregnant. She burst into tears, and as Fulton said afterwards 'carried on like one o'clock'.

Nevertheless she had the sense to see the sense in what they proposed, which was a great relief all round. 'Baby', as Patti's little bulge was referred to from now on, would have two fathers, mother would have two friends to help her bring it up, and they'd all have a nice big country house to live in, and Fulton would get out of Bath.

The house would have to be re-modelled, of course. There would be a wing for everyone, an Aga installed, and the Berber mottled replaced by polished boards and Persian rugs. Then a daily nanny would be engaged, because they all cried 'fains' to washing nappies. It was all going to be perfectly splendid, and just the sort of shot in the arm and change of circumstances that everyone could do with.

'Let's face it,' said Elliott, 'Fulton and I have been together for almost twenty years, and a late baby is just what the doctor ordered.'

After they had gone Patti took her little antique cushion, and went and sat under the old yew tree in the garden. She stared back at the house. She wanted to think about Gerard very much, as much as she could, because she had the feeling that very soon he would be fading away from her a little, and she wanted to think that he would think that it was all right, even though she knew that he would have a fit, about everything.

All the sights and the sounds of moving in, the fun she'd had with Gerard. It had all happened, and now more was to happen, but not with the same cast. She had never been one to worry much about the future, which was just as well, considering everything. Life had to be got through, the same way as when you were contracted for a show – it had to be got through. There was very little sense to it, no more than there had been to many of the shows she had danced in, but now and then, quiet happened, and you remembered things, all sorts of things, even the riding lessons, and you remembered them knowing that you might not be remembering them again, and there might not be ever that sort of time again.

No one in the village was to know about Baby, until after the solemnities. It was to be a secret wedding.

'As private as possible,' said Elliott, 'you know, just ourselves and the Press.'

The banns were to be read in Bath, because it was hoped that most of the congregation in Bath were too deaf to take any notice, and then they were all going to wear white, including Elliott, who was to be Queen of Honour, as well as Best Boyfriend, and the honeymoon was to be spent at Flint House, because the Bridal Couple had to redecorate all over again, because, as Fulton said, he was *not* ex-army and tenting was *not* his thing. Meanwhile Elliott would continue on his way, as previously planned, to Italy to trouvé antiques, and baby clothes exquisitely worked by nuns in hillside convents.

The bell, front, antique, and jarring, rang. Patti remembering Fulton and Elliott's precise instructions to keep herself as private as possible until the big day, opened one of the shutters that were nowadays always kept closed, and stared cautiously into the face of Mrs Dupont on the other side of the glass panel.

'Oh Mrs Dupont,' she said, 'I haven't seen you for months.' She did not open the door however.

'Well, I know,' said Mrs Dupont, 'but you know how it is, I've been *so* busy.'

'Well that's how it is,' said Patti smiling.

There was a small silence.

'May I come in?' asked Mrs Dupont, and rudely tried the handle of the front door at the same time.

'No,' said Patti.

'I'm sorry?'

'It's all right. I just don't want to see anyone at the moment.'

Patti closed the shutters again, and pulled the iron bar across them with some satisfaction. Not one of the village had bothered with her since she was widowed, and not one come to say 'hello', or pass the time of day, and now that she was to be married, and mistress of her own house again, she was not going to bother with any of them, not ever, and nor with the Hall, or with anyone, as a matter of fact. She had Fulton and Elliott now, and she could say two fingers to the rest of the world, and just have fun the way she wished. The way she had before Knightey went to heaven.

Mrs Dupont walked away rattling her collecting box in much the same way as a person who whistles aimlessly. There was no doubt about it, that had been a snub all right. The door had not been opened. The shutters hardly opened. She hurried towards her car, and aimed it at the Hall. Lady Pemberton should hear about this.

'What a darling he is,' said Mrs Dupont a little later staring into Jennifer's carriage-built pram with the Pemberton crest emblazoned on the side. Unfortunately the 'darling' was well covered up, and so it was not possible for her to see whether or not he was wearing the hand-crocheted bootees that she had made for him.

'Yes, such a good baby,' agreed Jennifer. 'And already so advanced.'

'Lord Pemberton must be so thrilled.'

'Yes. It has quietened his anxieties as far as the succession a great deal. It is now assured, as he says himself.'

'A great relief,' said Mrs Dupont patiently.

'A great relief,' agreed Jennifer.

Mrs Dupont was still standing, but Jennifer made no attempt to ask her to sit, so she did not feel that she could, but gave the carriage pram a little rock instead, as if she had not thought of sitting down, and wouldn't if she was asked. She sensed that Lady Pemberton was not in a good mood, and so she felt that she should say something.

'What a very pretty dress, Lady Pemberton,' she said.

'Don't rock the pram Jane, if you don't mind,' said Jennifer. 'He doesn't like it. And as for this dress, I hate it. It makes me feel very plain, but Lord Pemberton is in the mood to save, not on his racehorses, you must understand, but on items that *I* enjoy.'

Mrs Dupont was thrilled. She always loved hearing of the horrific deprivations of the very rich. The fact that 'they' had to make do was most gratifying. She had stopped rocking the pram, but since Jennifer had not asked her to sit down, and since she was in such a very bad mood, she remained standing, and smiled vacantly towards a flower bed.

Jennifer sighed.

'Lord Pemberton does not understand about women,' she said. 'He may like them, but he certainly doesn't understand them. He doesn't understand that they need clothes not just to look pretty, they need clothes so as not to look plain. I have always been plain. When I was little I was a plain child. People remarked on it quite loudly, you know. And then when I grew up people referred back to it; and now still older, and just a little less plain, people still talk about it, because they think it is quite safe to talk about it, because now I have cars, and clothes, and jewels, and they can hide the plainness quite comfortably; but you see I'm not better from the plainness. You never get better from it. Inside you are always – plain.'

Jennifer was now staring at the same flower bed as Mrs Dupont.

'That's why I need the clothes,' she added.

'Why doesn't Lord Pemberton want you to have them?'

'Cutbacks,' said Jennifer shortly. 'He has decided suddenly to "economise". Ridiculous. As if he can.'

'Oh dear, then I'm afraid I have called with my little collecting box at quite the wrong moment,' said Jane Dupont putting her marmalade jar back into her straw basket.

'By no means,' said Jennifer. 'What is it this time?'

'The Knitting Circle. Wool. It's soared.'

'Yes. Of course. Remind me when you leave.'

'As to "what is new" – I must tell you –'

Jennifer now patted the bench beside her, and Mrs Dupont felt able to sit down, a little thankfully because she was sinking into the lawn.

'As to what is new, you know "Patti" –'

'Our Bluebell. I haven't seen her for a long time I'm afraid.'

'Yes, well I called only a few minutes ago, and she refused to open to me. Now why do you think that could be?'

'Probably still in her nightdress, knowing that one.'

'No, she wasn't in her nightdress, but she did look most odd.'

'She always does.'

'Not "Bluebell" odd just ordinarily "odd".'

'How odd.'

'That's just what I thought.'

Jennifer looked thoughtful.

'Whatever it is that's making her odd the village will soon find out,' she said. 'You know the village.'

They knew the village, and as soon as 'it' found out that Patti had refused to open to Mrs Dupont, her telephone and doorbell sprang into life. Never since before Knightey had died, had she had so many callers. She took a great satisfaction in not answering to anyone. She would suffer her morning sickness undetected, as she had been left to suffer her mourning.

The following week she was picked up to drive to Bath to choose her wedding dress by 'the boys', both of whom were spending a fortune on their white wedding suits, even though, as they said themselves, they looked like strawberry vanilla gateaux in them.

Patti had never had a Church wedding before, and Fulton and she took a great interest in everything. There were no quarrels about the hymns, because having been to a convent Patti only knew 'God Bless the Pope', and none at all about the flowers, because Patti did not know anything about those either. It was a most unusually peaceful run-up to any marriage. In fact, the more Fulton realised just how little Patti knew about anything, the more he looked forward to the wedding. He would have an excuse at last, as her husband, to teach her taste as never before. His Lady Tizzy was going to be the epitome of taste – or 'epitomb' of taste, as she pronounced it. Not only that but he would be able to explain at last to her ladyship that 'eau de nil' was not bottled water, and dunking your biscuit was just *not* on.

The formalities must be observed to make things more exciting, and so Patti spent her last night as a single mother at Flint House, her wedding dress carefully laid out by Elliott, her flowers in the only little fridge that had been grudgingly left to her by Knightey's children. Her dress was so lovely that she couldn't sleep for stroking it. And occasionally when she wasn't stroking it, she thought about all she had to which she had to look forward, and had a cry, because she definitely didn't want to cry on the day, and ruin her make up.

The village was pottering about with small cans of weed spray when Patti's wedding car, complete with bridal streamers, drove gracefully through its small street, and up the hill towards her house. It was not a usual sight for a Saturday morning, and several of the early morning sprayers paused, only to do so again when the car returned, and it became perfectly plain to everyone that Lady Tisbury was the prospective bride, because she was sitting in the back wreathed in a Victorian lace jacket and dress, with a little hat with cream ostrich feathers perched upon her mountain of hair.

Jennifer heard from Jane Dupont of the sighting, and dropped the telephone to tell Pember, who was walking in the garden, principally because Jennifer was inside. As she came out to join him, he made to go in.

'Pember. Where are you going?'

'Going? I'm going into the village, that's where I'm going.'

'What for? You keep going into the village, but you never come back with anything.'

'No, I don't, do I?' agreed Pemberton. 'But this time I shall, I shall come back with something.'

'Jane Dupont has just seen Lady Tizzy sitting in the back of a wedding car dressed from top to toe as a bride. What do you think of that?'

'Jane Dupont is an ass.'

'Pember. Please. She's a friend of mine.'

'She's an ass.'

'But Pember, why do you think she should be getting married. She's only just been widowed.'

'People often do. Remarry. After a few months. It's quite normal. Can't stand being on their own. Although why I can't imagine. Goodness knows being on your own is preferable, in my mind, to being with someone who gets on your nerves.'

He gave a deep sigh.

'You know what I was thinking, Pember? I was thinking that she could be having a baby.'

'Now you're being an ass.'

'No really. She won't open to anyone. It must be a baby. Lady Tizzy's always been so forward. It's the only answer. She must be having a baby. Perhaps he left her pregnant, perhaps Sir G. left her pregnant?'

'He certainly didn't leave her anything else.'

'Oh but it couldn't be his, because he or she would be born by now. It must be someone *else's*.'

'This is just speculation.'

'No seriously, women have feelings about these sort of things – and I have a feeling.'

'Just because you're pregnant again you have to take everyone else down with you.'

'Oh Pember, we're really not getting on very well, are we?' asked Jennifer.

'I don't know what you mean.'

'That's what I mean.'

She walked off to find Nanny, who would believe every

word, particularly if it turned out not to be true.

'Just speculation,' said Pemberton again, but he sat down on Jennifer's bench and breathed deeply, even though he'd never been to Betty Parsons' relaxation classes.

Patti, given her condition, had been forced to rely upon Fulton choosing the 'right' guests for their wedding. Fulton, knowing the mirth his marriage would arouse, had chosen carefully, few but choice had been the theme, and so to join Elliott and turn the occasion into a party came Lucius, Hugo and Lady Mary.

'Most suitable,' said Elliott, 'since threesomes are so fashionable.'

The bridegroom cried a great deal more than anticipated during the service, so that it took much longer than it should. The vicar tried to speed things up, but without success. Hugo took tasteful pictures of the happy couple signing the registry, and then they all retired to the Francis Hotel for far too much champagne.

'The happiest of days,' said Elliott, before leaving for London with the other guests. 'Now don't dare to start on the wing before I get back. That's all I ask – leave the wing to me.'

'It was lovely, wasn't it?' said Patti, as they drove back to Flint House.

'I haven't cried so much since *Bambi*,' said Fulton.

They parked the car in front of Flint House, and then, to the complete fascination of half the village, Fulton was seen to pick up Lady Tizzy and carry her over her own threshold and into the house.

Once inside the dark of the hall Patti kissed Fulton, quite innocently, and Fulton kissed her back, without a trace of innocence.

'Goodness,' said Patti.

'Goodness has nothing whatever to do with it,' said Fulton.

They kissed again. And then after a long time, during which Fulton discovered that he was not all quite what he had always thought himself to be, he took her by the hand, and they ran upstairs to the bedroom.

'After all,' said Fulton, 'we are married!'

Chapter Thirteen

Andrew was being quite hopeless. The Countess could have strangled him. He had been drunk for over a fortnight. The dandruff on his British warm reminded her of the windowsills in London flats, so long caked with pigeon droppings that they had become crenellated.

She had asked him to her 'charity event' in aid of Georgiana, but was now regretting it dreadfully. He would ruin everything by talking about something that no one would want to listen to, or he would be drunk before anyone arrived. Or worst of all he would carry on about Lady Tizzy's marriage from the word go, and no one would know what he was talking about.

Every evening had been the same. He would arrive about five o'clock. Drink everything except the water in the flower vases, and then proceed to moan.

'How could she? And a man like that? I mean how could she?' he was moaning tonight.

'Women prefer men like that to men like you,' said the Countess. 'They're much easier to live with. They cook, and do the flowers and things. Men like you are such clots.'

'But she's so beautiful, it's such a waste.'

He stubbed his cigarette out in the stuffed olives.

'If I had known you were going to be so ridiculous about it all, I shouldn't have told you.'

'I should have found out, the Mu-Mu Maiden would have told me.'

'Personally I think you've gone senile.'

'She's so beautiful.'

Andrew was now sinking with the sun, a horizon of Colefax and Fowler feather-filled cushions rising to meet him.

The Countess sighed. She could only hope that tomorrow night, the night of the party, he would have either drunk himself into total unconsciousness, or that he would be too ill to attend, because he was quite obviously not going to be what Nanny would call a 'help'.

'Why don't you catch the last train to the country tonight?' she suggested.

'I can't. *She*'s there. The wretched, infernal, unspeakable woman.'

'Poor Clarissa. She's not quite as bad as you make out.'

'She's every bit as bad as I make out. She's as bad as anything you could think of. Worse.'

'I expect she's getting fed up with the country?'

'Not on your life. She loves the bloody place. She's joined everything except the Working Men's Club and the Rotarians. Horse Clubs, Pony Clubs, Gardening Clubs –'

'She's too old for the Pony Club –'

'Not Clarissa, she's taken over the sandwich-making section. She's even bought a special hat for judging tomatoes, and a pair of corduroy knickerbockers.'

'That is serious.'

'Serious? It's painful. From the back she looks like over-ripe greengages.'

'How's the house?'

'The house is a beast.'

'She should never have bought an "I see what you mean". I thought that might be a mistake.'

'What's a whatsisname?'

'An "I see what you mean" is a house which is a visual disappointment on the outside, with the result that the owner lavishes everything on the inside, as a consequence of which every time someone walks in they say "Oh, I see what you mean".'

'No this isn't that, this is an "I don't know what you mean". She can buy the one thing in a shop that is the only thing there that no one else would touch with a barge pole.'

'So you're no nearer a golden divorce?'

'Even further.'

'Nevertheless you must hold out. Perhaps she'll fall in love with a farmer?'

'She might, but he wouldn't, particularly not if he's dairy, he'll have enough cows already.'

'Even so I really think you ought to try and make that last train. Just for appearances.'

'Do you think so?'

Now he was becoming pathetic.

'I do. After all there is a bar. And all the porters will be drunk, because they always are, so you won't be conspicuous.'

She watched him staggering into a taxi, and then she closed the front door. She was exhausted. She would have to have a tray and telly, because tomorrow she must look her best for the 'charity event'.

She dressed slowly the following evening, because she was aware that everything must be right for Georgiana's sake, and she must not become flustered if something wasn't. There would have to be the right cross-section of people, the right amount of drinks, and the right people to serve as well as drink them. Among the guests would be a 'Lord Right', or at the very least an Hon. Something Right, and so everything would come right for Georgiana, even if it was a trifle tiring.

She was wearing Bellville-Sassoon, for the older woman. Elegant, softly flattering; she knew that she must look the perfect picture of arsenic in old lace.

Georgiana was looking breathtaking, which was gratifying since they were all going to such trouble for her. She was in deep blue, which made her eyes seem blue, which they weren't, and her long hair was drawn back at the sides to reveal a lovely pair of hooped diamond earrings, which belonged to the Countess. 'Kindly lent for the occasion.'

The party started well. So well that neither the Countess, nor Georgiana, noticed that James Stranragh had not arrived. When he did, he was almost late, but not quite, for Andrew, most unfortunately, had managed to remember, and arrived actually last of all, hot and tired off the early evening train. Fortunately he was only interested in getting 'stuck in', and didn't see the need to make conversation with anyone.

Stranragh was tall. The Countess liked a man to be tall. And he was handsome in a conventional way, not breathtakingly handsome like that silly little man that Mary had in tow, but handsome in a conventional way. He had a good head of hair that should be of the lasting kind, and he dressed well, but not so well that your suspicions as to his propensities were aroused. So, all in all, not a disappointment.

'No bog spavins! Not gone in the wind! Buy it!' her late husband would say.

Only one thing she didn't like. He had a little mouth. Still, you couldn't have everything, and if it meant that he was not profligate, that would not be a bad thing. Profligacy in a man was ridiculous, just as meanness in a woman was most unattractive.

She decided to introduce him to Georgiana later rather than sooner, but was saved the trouble, for after a decent interval he made his way across the room and introduced himself.

'Georgiana.' Stranragh had half-hoped to be disappointed. He had hoped that in her clothes she would be a trite recreation of the sensuous creature that he mentally possessed every night, but she was not.

He knew her voice would be important. Sometimes a girl could be neither beautiful, nor attractive, in repose and yet the moment she spoke her personality revved into life, and she would be instantly desirable. Other times the chassis would be sensational, but the motor itself dull and disappointing so that you weren't even tempted to take it for a spin. 'Georgiana' speaking was the same person that lay across his wall.

They talked of trivialities and then, since people were leaving and he had not arrived except towards the end, he asked her out to dinner.

'I'm not sure that I should dine with someone who knows what I look like without a stitch on,' she said, teasing him.

Until that moment she had not let him know that she knew who he was.

'Do you extend that rule to include the whole of the Royal Academy and their members?' he asked.

'Touché.'

She laughed, and he was glad to see that her laugh was not

disfiguring, but even so he wondered how she would eat? He so often hated to see women eat. He felt a great sympathy for Lord Byron who had insisted that the women in his life ate behind a screen. Seeing a woman eat could not but be a hurdle to desire, sometimes a barrier. Nevertheless he asked her out to dinner for he thought it was a hurdle that they should face straight away.

Georgiana accepted his invitation because she was hungry, and because he wore the right shirts, and the right suits, and had three houses.

From the window of her first-floor drawing room the Countess watched Stranragh hailing a cab for Georgiana, and then she allowed herself a little sigh.

'Very satisfying,' she said to a now comatose Andrew. 'Very satisfying indeed. Item one, give cocktail party for niece. Item two, invite eligible man. Item three, watch him take her out to dinner. Very satisfying.'

'Do stop matchmaking,' Andrew muttered. 'Look where it landed me.'

'Certainly not,' said the Countess. 'If I don't help Georgiana no one will. Besides, this one is most suitable. As to you, you have got everything you deserve, and you know it.'

She put out her arm to heave Andrew to his feet.

'Now we're going out to dinner, before you start making an ass of yourself.'

Andrew allowed himself to be pulled to his feet. 'You know,' he said, 'If I was younger, I'd marry you, you know that?'

The Countess laughed.

'I am a bit young for you, "old boy",' she agreed.

'Younger than most of the "girls" here tonight.'

'None so old as the young.'

'You're young like my mother was, she was always younger than everyone.'

'Yes, she was,' said the Countess, and she stopped for a moment remembering what a sweetie his mother had been.

Then they shut the door on the past, and went out to dinner.

If the Countess's matchmaking had afforded her satisfaction, and even a little amusement, Georgiana's first evening with James Stranragh afforded her neither.

He took her to a restaurant he obviously knew well. She did not like it. It was full of the kind of people who liked to dine quietly off menus complete with exactly the same kind of food that they eat at home. It had a depressing atmosphere. She felt that nothing exciting had ever happened there. No one had ever fallen in love across its tables, or caught sight of a beautiful face and got up to follow it. It had never heard a challenging remark, or listened to a great wit. It was stable and feed for unexceptional people. Altogether the effect was oppressive upon Georgiana, so that she was forced to spend the evening asking Stranragh about himself, and then pretending that his replies were fascinating, which they weren't. And while she appreciated the fact that he was a gentleman and held doors open for her, and even pulled out her chair for her (which she thought was excessive), nevertheless even his good manners bored her. Gus's ignorance of the niceties of social behaviour had amused her. His ability to walk ahead of her, forget to introduce her, and then remember to seduce her only when it suited him, had had the same effect upon her as being dragged to a cave. He had fascinated her in a way that she feared Stranragh never would.

They went back to his house for coffee. The address impressed. And although she did not like the icons in the hall, and the library was rather a dull grey, nevertheless the house offered great potential. It was too 'homme seul' of course, but that could always be changed.

While he was fetching the coffee she amused herself by mentally re-decorating the room. She rag-rolled the walls in a delicate yellow, and found just the right needlepoint rug for the centre of the floor, leaving a polished wood surround. She disarranged the books and put a bust upon the demi-lune, and some choice pieces of china – snuff boxes and so on. The curtains she put in a Grecian drape across a pole, and then allowed them to fall gracefully to the floor. She had such fun doing all this, that it was difficult not to feel impatient and cross when Stranragh re-appeared with coffee on a mahogany tray.

With the change of environment it was necessary to find new subjects to discuss. Georgiana chose Greece. And then she tired of little islands, and the Lion Gate, and switched to Scotland, because there was a picture of his house in Scotland over the

176

chimneypiece.

'I don't know Scotland,' she said.

They both knew what knowing Scotland meant. Nothing to do with the place itself, everything to do with the people who lived there, owned there, invited you there.

'It would suit you,' said Stranragh, meaning his house.

'It looks very wild and rugged,' she said ignoring him.

'It is very wild and rugged,' he admitted, and then seeing that she refused to understand him he asked if she would like to see the dining-room.

'Why? Are you still hungry?' she said mischievously.

'I have a painting I think you would like to see.'

They both knew which painting it was, although Georgiana did not know that Stranragh also owned the other one, and that it was hanging in his bedroom.

He noticed that she became animated rather than embarrassed when confronted by herself without her clothes, framed in heavy gold, and lit by a small picture light. The rest of the room was in darkness, so that the light from the picture only partially reflected upon her face, but he could feel her excitement, and he knew that it was because she was reminded of the painter. It made her manner change towards him almost immediately, as if they shared a secret, as if he had been present in the studio with her when the picture had been painted.

Seeing this Stranragh realised that she must never know that he had hired Hackett, and that he was even now living in his house in Italy. He had removed him effectively from her life, and he must remain removed. He also realised that it was essential to intrigue her, encourage her to confide in him, for he knew that he could not amuse her, he had seen that over dinner. She had tried too hard for him to be able to ignore her efforts.

She went home that night without him doing more than kiss her cheek.

'He's very nice,' she told the Countess next day over small glasses of medium-dry twelve o'clock sherry.

'Well. That's at least something,' said the Countess knowing that Georgiana would have liked to have added 'and dull'. 'Nice men are quite difficult to come by. Has he asked you out again?'

'Yes,' Georgiana lied.

In fact he did not telephone her again for a week, by which time she had forgotten that she thought he was nice and dull and was now prepared to see in him qualities that he did not possess, on the grounds that any man who could ignore her for a week must have admirable self-control and confidence, something which made him far from uninteresting in her eyes.

He took her to lunch. Not to the place that had previously bored her, but to a fashionable restaurant with pink tablecloths, where she amused them both by picking out couples lunching who should not be.

'Affair definitely,' she murmured discreetly every now and then, and Stranragh knew just from the way that she said those two words that she had had several lovers.

Perhaps because they now had his painting of her in common, she had stopped trying too hard, and treated him instead with an immediate intimacy that was flattering, and made her even more desirable. She touched him lightly on the arm, and laughed at his remarks in a charming way. He knew that she felt that she was in control of the situation, which meant that in his turn he could afford to be bold.

'I would like to buy you some clothes,' he said after lunch, offering her his arm.

She looked at him. She had been bought clothes by Kaminski. She was not unaware of the implications, and wondered what the Countess would advise her to do? But the Countess was not there, and Stranragh had already stopped in front of a shop which was known to sell clothes by some of her favourite designers.

'Why do you want to buy me clothes?' she asked. 'Don't you like mine?'

'Yes, I like yours, but I'd like to buy you anything you want. Everything you want.'

Georgiana ran up the steps of the shop in front of him. It was a long time since she had been bought beautiful things. Stranragh followed her slowly. He loved to see her legs in their stockings, and remind himself of how they looked without them.

In the shop she introduced herself to the assistant, and then found Stranragh a chair, in such a way that she made it appear that they had already been shopping together many times before. Stranragh was grateful for this even though it brought him to realise that a man buying her clothes was not a new experience. In the changing-room the assistant brought the clothes that he had chosen in to her. She was a dark-haired woman. Very slim and chic, with her heavy hair caught into a snood at her neck. She attended Georgiana's every change with love. Her beauty mesmerised them both.

'Not tall,' the assistant told her girlfriend later. 'But exquisitely made. A tiny waist, long legs, and a face of such innocence you knew she must be wicked.'

Stranragh's taste while conservative was, Georgiana had to admit, impeccable. He was also very patient, not seeming to mind the long delays between changes, the minutes that flowed past him before the assistant flung the changing-room curtain aside, and Georgiana stepped out for his appraisal.

He bought her everything that she wanted, and more than she wanted, so that his generosity was almost absurd.

'What shall I wear for you tonight?' she asked, teasing him, because he hadn't even mentioned 'tonight'.

'The blue,' he said. 'With the very tight waist.'

And then wished that he had told her that he was busy that night.

'Oh,' she replied, 'All right.'

And kissed him on the lips very much 'en passant' to her taxi.

Stranragh watched the cab driving away, and then without thinking particularly of where he was going he walked on towards his house, because he hated the idea of not seeing her again until the evening. He knew he was not the only man that had felt as he did about her, and the realisation that he was not the first, and that he might not be the last, was dreadful. The afternoon had been mesmeric. Each time the assistant had flung aside the curtain it seemed to him that she was stepping out to tempt him, and deny him. That she was mocking him, and the whole event, and at the same time anxiously seeking his approval.

'I hate her,' he told the dull grey sky.

He imagined her unwrapping everything that he had bought

her, and he wondered whether she would ring a girlfriend and boast a little of his generosity? And then he thought of her lying in her bath, her long hair swathed in a towel, her toe balanced upon the hot water tap. He knew what she would look like then, but he didn't know whether she would be thinking of him, mocking him, perhaps even believing that she had won? She had kissed him as you would kiss a child, and then she had left him as you would leave a child, watching after her, wondering.

He also realised that she had thought him dull until he had taken her to see 'Odalisque I' in the dining room, and then she had stopped thinking he was dull, and they had found that they had a shared secret in common, namely a mutual interest in her. He had punished her for that then, but now, after this afternoon, she had weakened his ability even to punish her. He wished he could hate himself, or both of them, or that he was not aware of his own dreadful unwillingness to release himself from his feelings.

'Well?'

She stood in the hall, a blue splash against the black and white marble floor, an absurd contrast to the icons behind her.

'Bring me the head of John the Baptist upon a plate,' he murmured.

'I'm sorry?'

'I think the belt could be tighter.'

'Oh.'

She stood in front of the Regency looking-glass. He stood behind her. She put her hands on her waist.

'Could you do it for me?'

'It would be better if you did it.'

'I can't,' said Georgiana truthfully. 'The buckle's one of those rather stiff ones.'

She turned and faced him. Stranragh looked down at the belt, and then at her. Now she was laughing at him. He pulled on the belt.

'Now I can't breathe at all,' she said.

'I thought we should have dinner here tonight,' he said, holding open the library door.

'Please don't talk about dinner. I shall certainly faint if I even see a plate,' she said. But she made no move to unbuckle the belt.

180

He had a bottle of champagne standing in a wine cooler, because she had told him how much she liked to drink champagne.

He poured it into chilled glasses, which although probably correct seemed to her just a little old-maidish.

'There should be a toast,' she said.

'There is.'

He raised his glass.

'To the Odalisques.'

He saw immediately how much it meant to her that he should admire her body, worship her form.

'You haven't got both?' she asked surprised.

'But of course.'

'Where is the other one? I haven't seen the other one.'

More memories, he thought, more memories of those days.

'I'll show you – after dinner.'

He served her, and she let him, sitting quite still in her mahogany chair with its arms shaped into swans' heads. By now she felt quite faint from the tightness of the belt, but she would not loosen it. She was too vain to let him see that it hurt, and that her waist was not as small as he would perhaps like it to be. She knew now that he could not be as dull as she had at first imagined, for a dull man would not have bought two nudes of her. It was an excess which was flamboyantly flattering.

'I love secrets,' she said, à propos of nothing at all.

The dinner had been left under silver covers. It was unexceptional, although the wine was superb. She felt she had no need to eat a great deal since he would not have cooked it.

After dinner she played the piano. He would have liked her to play Bach. She played Chopin. He watched her much as Kaminski used to watch her, as if he was saving her up. She played what is known as 'charmingly'.

'You play beautifully.'

'Only the few pieces I know well. My repertoire is tiny.'

He stood up.

'Shall I take you to see the other painting now?'

Georgiana smiled.

'It's in my bedroom.'

'I think you're really Bluebeard, really,' she said following him up the stairs.

The bedroom, his bedroom, had suede-lined walls, brown suede-lined walls, and a chrome bed with a fur rug. It was even more 'homme seul' than the library. Georgiana knew that if she opened one of the cupboards she would see dozens of the striped shirts that Stranragh favoured for London, and rows of the black shoes that he was now occupying, and that there would be the slight smell of rust and pepper that she always associated with men's wardrobes.

'Odalisque II' was opposite his bed, exactly opposite. When she saw it Georgiana laughed, not with embarrassment, but with a kind of delight.

'I suppose that's just about the only place that you could hang it,' she said.

'What do you think of when you look at it?'

'Love,' she said simply, 'what else?'

She sat down suddenly on the bed.

'It's no good,' she said, 'I've got to give in.'

Stranragh looked at her astonished.

'The belt,' she said. 'It's far too tight. You'll have to undo it.'

He leant forward to undo it. His signet ring rang briefly against the buckle.

'Thank you,' she said, 'that's much better.'

He turned away from her dressed and looked at the painting of her naked. As she re-did the buckle with some difficulty, he kept his back tactfully turned around, much as a man might do with someone undressing on a beach.

'Thank you.'

Georgiana stood up. But Stranragh remained staring at the painting. She waited for one more moment, then left the room without him.

He went away to Italy for a week. He saw Hackett. His work on the hall was progressing satisfactorily. It would take longer than he supposed, he told Stranragh, who did not seem displeased by this. Hackett was living with a local girl. She had the long blonde hair, and brown eyes of an almond colour that is typical in Umbria. She was modelling one of the faces of the Vestal Virgins in the fresco. She was also a nymphomaniac, Hackett told

182

Stranragh with some satisfaction.

For some reason that he could not understand in himself, Stranragh felt offended by Hackett's ability to find sexual satisfaction so quickly after Georgiana. The fact that she had had an affair with a man who could turn from her to someone else so easily seemed to make her slightly less in his eyes, until he reminded himself that painters were different. Sex was light, food, and drink to them. Even so, he was prepared to find, on his return, that what he had felt for Georgiana might have lessened, or that there might be something coarse in her manner, something that he had not noticed before, something to suggest that she was not the girl in his paintings, but someone more akin to the sexual puppet with whom Hackett had taken up.

He waited a few days after his return to London before he rang her, and when he did he found himself half-hoping that she would be different, so that he could be released from his obsession. It was absurd to feel disappointed that she sounded more than ever the 'Odalisque', but he did, disappointed and amazed that this illness from which he was suffering would not be cured. She agreed to come to dinner with him, but he sensed that her pleasure that he had rung her was being checked by the humiliation that she felt that he had not rung her sooner.

He loved to watch people unobserved, so he waited for her to arrive hidden by the library curtain. How would it seem to him that she was, if he did not know her? If, casually, by chance, he watched her as a stranger would watch her? Would he then feel as he did?

As a stranger, or as himself, he found that he became mesmerised by her as soon as she stepped out of the taxi. Fragile in the crude light of the street lamp, wearing something that he had bought her that day in Beauchamp Place, he felt at once jealous of her, and jealous over her. His obsession with her had returned even before he opened the door.

'I've missed you,' she said, going to kiss him.

He turned away from her so that she wouldn't see the effect that her kiss had upon him.

'I've been very busy – since I got back.'

She looked up at him.

'Stranragh – what is it?'

He turned away and went back into the library ahead of her.

'Why do you never call me "James"?'

'Because you're Stranragh.'

She rolled the 'rrs' with exaggerated delight, and he had the feeling that once again, in spite of everything that he had done to prove to her that he was stronger than she imagined, she was once more eluding him, staying just out of his reach.

'They have beautiful jewellery in Florence,' he said, as if breaking a long silence and introducing a new subject to relieve the tension.

He gave her a box. Inside was a beautiful piece wrought delicately, gold like spiders' webs, tiny tactful jewels.

'How clever of you.'

She put up her hand to touch his cheek, and he knew that she was pleased, and that she loved what he could give her, and that she was patronising him.

She looked so frail, and yet he saw that she was in fact strong, not weakened by passion as he was. He longed to ask her to say that she loved him, and yet he couldn't bring himself to ask her to say that she did, because he knew she would say not 'I love you', as he wanted it said, but 'of course I love you' – in a surprised, or mischievous way, that would leave him as much in doubt as before.

Georgiana reached up and put her arms round him, and kissed him as if she knew that it was expected of her.

'You know that I want to marry you, don't you?' he said.

Georgiana nodded. She understood that Stranragh was not only a lord, but also a gentleman, because he was treating her with respect, the kind of respect of which Nanny would approve. It had come to matter very much to her that Stranragh would propose. Taking a lover such as Kaminski was colourful, having an affair with a painter was excusable, but a long association with someone from her own background would be humiliating. There had come to be no question in her mind but that Stranragh would propose and that she would accept, and that in doing so she would not only save Longborough, but gain the approval of everyone.

While he was away in Italy she had shut herself in her flat for hours dreaming of her future existence, an existence that she knew was possible because she saw it reflected in all the fashion magazines that she bought. She knew Stranragh loved her, and would give her everything that she wanted, and she had come to realise that this was an acceptable alternative to the kind of love that she had felt for Kaminski, or that Gus had finally felt for her. Possibly because of this, she now had a feeling of merely re-living what had already taken place. And it was hardly surprising, for as she looked up at Stranragh and told him that she accepted that he not only wanted to marry her, but that she would marry him, she had already mentally designed a new wardrobe for herself, commissioned a portrait 'after Winterhalter' (white evening dress draped with a sash of the Stranragh tartan) to hang above the chimneypiece, and bought herself a perfect pony and trap in which to trot around his estates.

'We do love each other, don't we?' she said, kissing him again.

'It must be faced,' the Countess said a few months later. 'Weddings are really rather bourgeois. Too reminiscent of camels loaded with silver plodding through mountain passes.'

She stared at the five boxes of silver spoons which had been sent to her address at various intervals for Georgiana.

To an outsider, however, the wedding of Lady Georgiana Longborough to the Third Baron Stranragh was on the contrary everything that it ought to be. It was to be held at the family seat, the service was to be conducted in the family chapel, the bride was to wear the family tiara, and be attended by innumerable and perfectly costumed 'smalls', all of them offspring of friends of the family. There was a large guest list, with on the bride's side of the Church, Society well represented, racing somewhat less, and the Arts not at all. On the bridegroom's side, art, motor racing and 'Scotland' were strongly in evidence.

The Marquis and Marchioness of Pemberton were pleased to attend on the bride's side. They sent a rose bowl as a gift, and the Marchioness took great trouble to let it be known how pleased she was for her old friend, particularly since she had been tactful enough not to marry better, always endearing in a girlfriend. Other guests on the bride's side were the Hon. Andrew Gillott, standing beside the Countess and well away from his wife, the former Mrs Parker-Jones. Lady Mary was there in mauve, as were the two men with whom she now shared her life, and who, as Andrew later remarked at the reception, '*should* have been in mauve.'

Last to arrive, and only just before the bride and her father, was Fulton, bearing Lady Tizzy on his arm with great pride. His new wife's advanced state of expectant motherhood was all too evident.

'Well,' announced the Countess. 'If you believe that you'll believe anything.'

The bride herself looked beautiful, radiant and serene, as any girl must who knows she is doing the right thing.

The press, however, were not greatly intrigued. Lady Georgiana Longborough marrying an unsuitable artist was news. Lady Georgiana Longborough marrying back into *Debrett* was not.

The honeymoon was to have been spent in Kenya. But at the last minute Stranragh cancelled it, much to Georgiana's dismay, and instead took her straight to his house in Scotland. Which was where Georgiana discovered her husband's true nature. And once she had discovered it, she found herself longing for Gus, whose way with her had at least been born of love. Nevertheless, she recognised that Stranragh, and the life to which she was now committed with him, was exactly what she deserved.